Amealia Jewett

THE
CAT WHO SAW STARS

Also by Lilian Jackson Braun

THE CAT WHO READ BACKWARDS
THE CAT WHO ATE DANISH MODERN
THE CAT WHO TURNED ON AND OFF
THE CAT WHO SAW RED
THE CAT WHO PLAYED BRAHMS
THE CAT WHO PLAYED POST OFFICE
THE CAT WHO KNEW SHAKESPEARE
THE CAT WHO SNIFFED GLUE
THE CAT WHO WENT UNDERGROUND
THE CAT WHO TALKED TO GHOSTS
THE CAT WHO LIVED HIGH
THE CAT WHO KNEW A CARDINAL
THE CAT WHO MOVED A MOUNTAIN
THE CAT WHO WASN'T THERE
THE CAT WHO WENT INTO THE CLOSET
THE CAT WHO CAME TO BREAKFAST
THE CAT WHO BLEW THE WHISTLE
THE CAT WHO SAID CHEESE
THE CAT WHO TAILED A THIEF
THE CAT WHO SANG FOR THE BIRDS

**THE CAT WHO HAD 14 TALES
(SHORT STORY COLLECTION)**

LILIAN JACKSON BRAUN

THE
CAT WHO SAW STARS

DOUBLEDAY DIRECT LARGE PRINT EDITION

G. P. Putnam's Sons
New York

This large Print Edition, prepared especially for Doubleday Inc., contains the complete unabridged text of the original publisher's Edition.

G. P. Putnam's Sons
Publishers Since 1838
a member of
Penguin Putnam Inc.
375 Hudson Street
New York, NY 10014

ISBN: 0-7394-0160-2

Printed in the United States of America

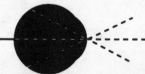

This Large Print Book carries the Seal of Approval of N.A.V.H.

Dedicated to Earl Bettinger,
The Husband Who . . .

THE
CAT WHO SAW STARS

1

World-shaking news was seldom broadcast by WPKX, the radio station serving Moose County, 400 miles north of everywhere. Local baseball scores, another car accident, a fire in a chicken coop, and death notices were the usual fare. In late June, listeners snapped to attention, then, when a Sunday evening newscast included this bulletin:

"An unidentified backpacker of no known address may or may not be a missing person, according to Moose County authorities. The Caucasian male, thought to be in his early twenties, stowed his camping gear on private property in the Fishport area three days ago and has not returned. He is described as fair-haired with blue eyes and of medium build. When last seen, he was wearing cut-off jeans, a white T-shirt, and a camera on a neck strap. Anyone seeing an individual of this description should notify the sheriff's department."

Since the description might fit any number of vacationers in Moose County, the listening audience ignored the matter until the next day, when it was reported in the local newspaper. A detailed story—written in folk-style by Jill Handley, feature editor of the *Moose County Something*—made sense of the incident.

Where's David?

MISSING HIKER
BAFFLES F'PORT
by Jill Handley

Magnus Hawley of Fishport, a veteran on the commercial fishing boats, flagged down a sheriff's patrol car on Sunday and told a curious tale. Hawley and his wife, Doris, live in a trailer home surrounded by flower beds on Lakeshore Road near Roaring Creek.

"T'other night," Hawley said, "me and m'wife had just ate supper and was watchin' TV when there come a knock on the door. I goes to the door, and it's a young feller with a big backpack, wantin' to pitch his tent down by the crick for a coupla nights. He says he's gonna do some hikin' on the beach. He's kinda sweaty and dusty, y'know, but he has a reg'lar haircut and talks decent."

Doris Hawley approved of the stranger. "He reminded me of our grandson—nice smile, very polite. I asked if he would be hunting for agates on the beach, because I could suggest a good spot, but he said he was mostly interested in taking pictures. His camera looked expensive, and I thought maybe he was a professional photographer. We told him he could camp near the picnic table at the bottom of the hill, so long as he didn't throw trash in the creek or play loud music."

The stranger said his name was David. "I never knew a David who wasn't trustworthy," she said.

She gave him some of her home-made ginger snaps and filled a jug with fresh water from the well. Her husband told David it was okay to take a dip in the creek but warned him about slippery rocks and strong current. Shortly after, they saw the young man heading for the lakeshore with his camera.

"Funny thing, though," said Hawley. "After that we di'n't see hide or hair of the feller. I went down to the crick in a coupla days to see if he'd cleared out. The water jug—it was still on the picnic table, full up! And his pack was underneath, all strapped and buckled. On'y thing gone was the cookies. We talked about it, Doris and me. I said he could've took up with somebody he met on the beach. There's no tellin' what kids'll do these days, y'know. But m'wife was worried about him slippin' on the rocks and gettin' drowned, so I hailed the patrol car."

A sheriff's deputy and a state trooper inspected the campsite but found no identification of any kind. A description of the hiker, as given by the Hawleys, was broadcast Sunday night, but no response to the bulletin had been received at press time.

Following the appearance of the story, the local gossip mill started grinding out

idle speculations and inventing sensational details. Abduction was a possibility,
many said, nodding their heads wisely. A
few busybodies suspected the Hawleys of
foul play. "Don't eat any ginger snaps" was
the popular quip in bars and coffee shops.

One who listened to the gossip without
contributing to it was Jim Qwilleran, a long-
time journalist now writing a twice-weekly
column for the *Something*. Only recently he
had interviewed Hawley and other commercial fishermen, even spending time on
the lake with a hard-working crew and a
half-ton of slippery fish, and he resented
the malicious whispers. Yet, that was to be
expected in a community polarized between boaters and landlubbers. Qwilleran's
own reaction to the backpacker's disappearance was an educated curiosity. For-
merly a crime reporter in major cities
around the United States, he had retained
a Sherlockian interest in solving mysteries.

Qwilleran was a popular man-about-
town in Pickax City, the county seat (popu-
lation 3,000). His column, "Straight from
the Qwill Pen," was said to rate ninety
percent readership—more than the daily
horoscope. Wherever he went in the

county, he drew attention, being a good-looking fifty-plus and a well-built six-feet-two with a moustache of outstanding proportions. It had a droop that accentuated his melancholy demeanor, and his eyes had a brooding intensity. Yet friends knew him to be amiable, witty, willing to do favors, and fond of taking them to dinner.

There was something else in Qwilleran's favor: He was a philanthropist of incredible generosity. Earlier in life he had been a hard-working journalist Down Below, as locals called the high-population centers around the country. He lived from paycheck to paycheck with no thought of accumulating wealth. Then a happenstance that was stranger than fiction made him the most affluent individual in the northeast central United States; he inherited the Klingenschoen estate. The fortune had been amassed when the area was rich in natural resources and no one paid income tax. As for the original Klingenschoen, he had operated a highly profitable business.

To Qwilleran the very notion of all that money was a burden and actually an embarrassment . . . until he thought of establishing the Klingenschoen Foundation.

Now financial experts at "the K Fund" in Chicago managed the fortune, distributing it for the betterment of the community and leaving him free to write, read, dine well, and do a little amateur sleuthing. Townfolk of every age and income bracket talked about him at clubs, on the phone, in supermarkets. They said:

"Swell fella! Not stuck up at all. Always says hello. Never know he was a billionaire."

"He sure can write! His column's the only thing in the paper I ever read."

"That's some moustache he's got! M'wife says it's sexy, 'specially when he wears sunglasses."

"Wonder why he stays single. They say he lives in a barn—with two cats."

"You'd think he'd get a proper house—and a dog—even if he doesn't want a wife."

Qwilleran's oversized moustache was a virtual landmark in Moose County, admired by men and adored by women. Like his hair, it was turning gray, and that made it more friendly than fierce. What no one knew about was its peculiar sensitivity. Actually, it was the source of his hunches. Whenever faced with suspicious circumstances, he felt a nudge on his upper lip that prompted him to start asking questions. Frequently he could be seen patting his moustache or grooming it with his fingertips or pounding it with his knuckles; it depended on the intensity of the nudge. Observers considered the gesture a nervous habit. Needless to say, it was not something Qwilleran cared to explain—even to his closest friends.

With the disappearance of the backpacker, a nagging sensation on his upper lip was urging him to visit Fishport, a modest village near the resort town of Mooseville, where he had a log cabin and a half-mile of lake frontage. The cabin, part of his inheritance, was small and very old but adequate for short stays in summertime. Only thirty miles from Pickax, its remoteness was more psychological than geographic. Mooseville, with its hundred miles of lake for a vista, and with its great dome of sky, was a different world. Even the pair of Siamese with whom he lived responded to its uniqueness.

A propitious fate had brought the three of them together. The female had been a poor little rich cat abandoned in a posh neighborhood when Qwilleran found her.

Because of her sweet expression and winning ways, he named her Yum Yum. The sleek muscular male had simply moved in—at a time when Qwilleran was trying to get his life together. Kao K'o Kung had been his name before being orphaned. Now called Koko, he had a magnificent set of whiskers and remarkable sensory attributes. In fact, he and Qwilleran had developed a kind of kinship—the one with a feline radar system and the other with an intuitive moustache.

The day after the newspaper story about the backpacker, Qwilleran drove downtown to the *Something* office to announce his vacation plans and hand in his copy for the "Qwill Pen" column. He had written a thousand words about the Fourth of July from the viewpoint of Benjamin Franklin. (How would Poor Richard react to backyard barbecues and high school majorettes in silver tights?) He found the managing editor's office decorated with crepe-paper streamers and a sign daubed with the message: HAPPY BIRTHDAY, JUNIOR . . . TODAY YOU ARE 16! Junior Goodwinter was past thirty, but slight stature and boyish features gave him the look of a perennial schoolboy.

"Happy sixteenth!" Qwilleran said. "You don't look a day over fifteen!" Dropping into a chair, he propped his right ankle on his left knee. "Any coffee left?"

The editor swiveled in his chair and poured a mugful. "Did you see our story on the backpacker, Qwill? A teacher in Sawdust City called and laid us out for quoting the fisherman verbatim instead of correcting his grammar. What we printed is exactly how he said it. Jill had it all on tape."

"Pay no attention. She's a crank," Qwilleran said. "There's nothing wrong with a little local color to relieve the monotony of good English."

"I'm with you," Junior said. "Then a guy called and complained because Hawley's wife was quoted as speaking better than her husband. He called it gender bias."

"I've met them both! That's the way they speak, for Pete's sake! I'm glad I don't have your job, Junior."

"The Sawdust City woman wants us to start running a column on correct speech instead of 'wasting so much space on sports.' I quote."

"No one would read it."

"It would have to be chatty, like Ann Landers . . . Well, anyway, what are you doing for the Fourth?"

"Leaving for a month's vacation at the beach."

"Are you taking the cats?"

"Of course! The beach is Cat Heaven! The screened porch is their Cloud Nine! I go up there for peace and quiet. They go for sounds and sights: squawking gulls, peeping sandpipers, cawing crows, chipping chipmunks! And everything moves: birds, butterflies, grasshoppers, waving beach grass, splashing waves . . ."

"Sounds like fun," Junior said. "And what will you be doing?"

"Reading, loafing, biking, walking on the beach . . ."

"Can you file your copy from up there?"

"What?"

"Does anyone have a fax machine you can use?"

"You forget I'm going on vacation. I haven't had one since God-knows-when."

"But you know the readers have fits if your column doesn't run . . . And you boast you can write it with one hand tied behind your back."

"Well . . . only because it's your birthday."

"Did you read Jill's piece about the new restaurant up there?"

"Yes, and I'm looking forward to checking it out. The new summer theater, too."

"Friday is opening night," Junior said. "How'd you like to review the play for us?" He caught Qwilleran's dour glance. "I know it's your vacation, but you're a writer, and writers write—the way other people breathe. How about it, Qwill? You can review a play blindfolded."

"Well . . . I'll think about it."

Before leaving the building, Qwilleran stopped in the publisher's office. He and Arch Riker had been lifelong friends and fellow journalists Down Below. Both had adapted to country living, but Arch had gone so far as to marry a local woman. Now his naturally florid face glowed with midlife contentment, and his paunchy midriff was getting paunchier. Mildred Riker was food writer for the paper.

Qwilleran asked, "Have you two moved to your beach house?"

"Sure have! It's a longer commute but worth it. There's something about the lake air that's invigorating."

And intoxicating, Qwilleran thought; the locals are all a little balmy, and the summer people soon get that way. He said, "I'm packing up the cats and moving up there myself this afternoon. Polly will be gone all month, you know."

Riker had his Mildred, and Qwilleran had his Polly Duncan. She was the director of the Pickax Public Library, and the possibility of their marriage was widely discussed in the community. Both preferred their individual lifestyles, however, and let it be known that their cats were incompatible.

Riker said, "Why don't you come and have dinner with us tonight? The Comptons will be there, and Mildred is doing her famous coddled pork chops."

"What time?"

"About seven . . . What do you think about the Fishport mystery? Have you heard the rumor about the Hawleys?"

"Yes, and I won't dignify it with a comment."

"Personally," Riker said, "I think it's all a publicity stunt trumped up by the chamber of commerce to promote tourism."

Qwilleran could never leave downtown without stopping at the used book store. He collected preowned classics as others in his financial bracket collected Van Goghs. Currently he was interested in Mark Twain. Coming from bright sunlight into the gloomy shop, he saw dimly. There was movement on a tabletop; that was Winston, the dust-colored longhair, flicking his tail over the biographies. There were sounds in the back room and the aroma of frying bacon; that was Eddington Smith preparing his lunch.

A bell had tinkled on the door, and the old gray bookseller came out eagerly to meet a customer. "Mr. Q! I've found three more for you, all with good bindings: *Connecticut Yankee, A Horse's Tale*, and *Jumping Frog*. Mark Twain lectured up here once, my father told me, so his books were popular. Two or three show up in every estate liquidation."

"Well, keep your eyes peeled for the titles I want, Ed. I'm going on vacation for a few weeks."

"Do you have plenty to read? I know you like Thomas Hardy, and I just found a leatherbound edition of *Far from the Madding Crowd.* My father used that expression often, and I never knew that he got it from Thomas Hardy."

"Or Thomas Gray," Qwilleran corrected him. "Gray said it first—in *Elegy Written in a Country Churchyard.*"

"I didn't know that," said Eddington, always glad to learn a new fact. "I'll tell my father tonight when I talk to him." Then he added in response to a questioning glance, "I talk to him every night and tell him the events of the day."

"How long has he been gone?" Qwilleran asked.

"He died peacefully in his sleep fourteen years ago next month. We were in the book business together for almost forty years."

"A rare privilege." Qwilleran had never known his own father. He bought the Thomas Hardy book as well as the others and was leaving the store with his purchases when the bookseller called after him. "Where are you going on vacation, Mr. Q?"

"Just up to Mooseville."

"That's nice. You'll see some flying saucers."

Qwilleran bristled at the suggestion but said a polite maybe. Both he and Arch Riker, professional skeptics, scoffed at the UFO gossip in Mooseville. The chamber of commerce encouraged it, hoping for an incident that would make the town the Roswell of the North. Tourists were excited at the prospect of seeing aliens. Friendly locals referred to them as Visitors; others blamed them for every quirk of weather or outbreak of sheep-fly. Qwilleran, to his dismay, had found several believers in the interplanetary origin of UFOs—among such persons as Riker's wife, the superintendent of schools, and a sophisticated young heiress from Chicago . . . or else they were playacting to preserve a local tradition, like adults pretending to believe in Santa Claus.

The last stop on his morning round was Amanda's design studio, where Fran Brodie, second in command, was back from vacation. She was one of the most attractive young women in Pickax, as well as one of the most talented, and now she had the added glamor that seems to come with foreign travel.

He said, "I don't need to ask if you had a good time. You look spectacularly happy."

"It was fabulous!" she cried, tossing her strawberry-blond hair. "Have you been to Italy?"

"Only as a foreign correspondent for papers Down Below."

"You must go there for a vacation and take Polly! The cities! The countryside! The art! The food! The people!" She rolled her eyes in a way that suggested she was not telling the whole story about . . . *the people.* "Sit down, Qwill, we have things to discuss."

She had done a small design job for him and was redesigning the interior of the Pickax Hotel, but her greatest passion was the Pickax Theater Club. It had been her idea to do summer theater in a barn near Mooseville. They were opening with a comedy, *Visitor to a Small Planet.*

"Are you going to review our opening night, Qwill?"

"I'm afraid so."

"For the first time in club history we're getting reviewers from neighboring counties: the *Lockmaster Ledger* and *Bixby Bugle*! Do you know the play?"

"Only that Gore Vidal wrote it and it opened on Broadway a long time ago."

"It's a fun production," Fran said. "A flying saucer lands in front of a TV commentator's house, and a Visitor from outer space proceeds to stir things up."

"Who's playing the Visitor? Were you able to draw from a pool of small green actors?"

"That's our big joke, Qwill. We've purposely cast actors under five-feet-nine for all the earthlings, so the Visitor comes as a shock. He's six-feet-eight!"

"Derek Cuttlebrink!"

"Isn't that a hoot? Larry's playing the commentator, and Scott Gippel is perfect for the overbearing general . . . Shall I have two tickets at the box office for you on Friday?"

"One will do," Qwilleran said. "Polly's vacationing with her sister in Ontario. They're seeing Shakespeare in Stratford and some Shaw plays at Niagra-on-the-Lake."

"Oh, I'm envious!" Fran cried.

"Don't be greedy! You've just seen the Pope in Rome, David in Florence, and all those virile gondoliers in Venice."

She gave him a Fran Brodie glance—half amusement, half rebuke.

"Where did you find a barn suitable for a theater?" he asked.

"Avery Botts is letting us use his dairy barn for nine weekends. Each play will run three weekends."

"I see," said Qwilleran thoughtfully. "And what will the cows do on weekends?"

"Are you serious, Qwill? Avery quit dairy farming a long time ago, when the state built the prison. They gave him a lot of money for his back forty, and he switched to poultry. You must have seen his place on Lakeshore just west of Pickax Road: big white frame farmhouse with a lot of white outbuildings. A sign on the lawn says: FRESH EGGS . . . FRYERS. Avery tells a funny story about that. Want to hear it?"

"Is it clean?"

"Well, one summer day," she began, "a city dude and a flashy blonde drove into the farmyard in a convertible with the top down. The guy yelled that he wanted a dozen fryers. Avery told him he had only three on hand but could have the other nine in a couple of hours. The guy slammed into reverse and yelled, 'Forget

it! Sell your three eggs to somebody else!'
And he gunned the car back down the
drive in a cloud of dust. When Avery tells
the story, he laughs till he chokes."

"I don't get it," Qwilleran admitted, "but
I'm a city dude myself."

"A fryer, Qwill, is a young chicken—not
an egg that you fry!"

"Hmmm . . . learn something every day."

"We're going to call our theater the Fryers Club Summer Stage . . . But I'm doing
all the talking," she said. "What's your
news?"

"Only that the cats and I are moving to
the beach for a month."

"Have you seen your new guest
house?"

"Not yet. I hope you didn't make it too
comfortable or too attractive. I don't want
to find myself in the motel business."

"Don't worry. I did it in bilious colors with
lumpy mattresses, flimsy towels, and
framed pictures of drowning sailors."

"Good!" he said. "See you Friday night.
Break a leg!"

Driving back to the barn to collect the
Siamese for the Mooseville expedition,

Qwilleran considered what he would need to pack in his van. For himself it would be, first of all, the automated coffeemaker. Otherwise he would require only polo shirts, shorts, and sandals, plus writing materials and a few books. There was no point in taking the revolutionary high-tech recumbent bike that had been presented to him by the community as a token of their esteem. The rider reclined in a bucket seat, pedaling with elevated feet. Needless to say, it was such a sensation in Pickax that he seldom ventured out on the highway; instead he displayed it in his living room as a conversation piece and even an art object. On this occasion, he decided to leave it where it was; after all, there was a trail bike in the toolshed at the cabin.

The cats' vacation needs were more complex. He would have to take their blue cushion from the top of the refrigerator; the turkey roaster that served as their commode; several bags of their favorite cat litter that was kind to the toes; grooming equipment; their special dishes for food and water; a month's supply of Kabibbles, a crunchy treat prepared by a neighbor; and a few cans of their preferred brands of red salmon, crabmeat, lobster, and smoked turkey.

Right now it was time for their midday snack, and they would be waiting for him, prancing on long thin legs, waving eloquent tails, raising eager eyes that were pools of blue in their brown masks. When he unlocked the door, however, both were asleep on the sofa—a tangle of pale fawn fur and brown legs and tails, with heads buried in each other's underside, except for three visible ears.

"Treat!" he said in a stage whisper.

Two heads popped up!

"Yow!" came Koko's clamoring response.

"N-n-now!" shrieked Yum Yum.

After the luggage was packed and the van loaded, and after Yum Yum had been chased and captured and pushed into the cat carrier, Koko was found sitting in the bucket seat of the recumbent bike, looking wise.

Oh, well, Qwilleran thought; I might as well take it along. I can practice on the back roads.

2

The two passengers in the cat carrier on the backseat complained and jockeyed for position, then settled down as the brown van picked up speed on the open highway. The route to Mooseville lay due north. For Qwilleran, it was a highway of memories, crowded with landmarks from his earlier experiences in the county:

Dimsdale Diner (bad coffee, good gossip) . . . Ittibittiwassee Road (turn left to Shantytown, right to the Buckshot Mine) . . . old turkey farm (once owned by Mildred Riker's first husband) . . . abandoned cemetery (poison ivy) . . . state prison (famous flower gardens, infamous scandal).

At the prison gates, the dozing Siamese perked up, stretched their necks, and sniffed. It was not roses they smelled; it was the lake, still a mile away. They detected open water, aquatic weeds, algae, plankton, minnows!

Their excitement increased as the van traveled along the lakeshore road. On the left, Qwilleran saw Avery Botts's farmhouse and the Fryers Club Summer Stage . . . on the right, glimpses of the lake between the trees . . . on the left, pastureland with cattle ruminating or horses showing off their glossy coats and noble bearing . . . on the right, the rustic gate of Top o' the Dunes Club, where the Rikers had their beach house . . . on the left, a solitary stone chimney, all that remained of an old one-room schoolhouse . . . on the right, the letter K on a post.

This was the old Klingenschoen property, a half-square mile of ancient forest on ancient sand dunes, with a sandy drive winding among pines, oaks, maples, and cherry trees. After dipping up and down aimlessly, it emerged in a clearing where a cabin overlooked a hundred miles of water. Built of full-round logs interlocking at the corners, the small cabin seemed anchored to the ground by its enormous stone chimney. Eighty-foot pine trees with only a few branches at the top surrounded it like sentinels.

Before bringing the cats indoors, Qwilleran inspected the premises, which had been cleaned and summerized by a youthful maintenance crew called the Sand Giant's Gnomes. The interior space was limited: a single large room with two cubicles at one end and a stone fireplace spanning the other. What suggested spaciousness and a kind of grandeur was the open ceiling that soared to the peak of the roof and was crisscrossed by log beams and braces. As soon as blinds were opened, the large window facing the lake and the three new skylights in the roof filled the interior with shafts of light.

Only then was the carrier brought indoors, its occupants jostling roughly and yowling loudly. The tiny door was unlatched, and suddenly they were quiet and wary.

"It's safe!" Qwilleran reassured them. "No lions or tigers! The floor has been cleaned and polished, and you can walk on it with impunity." The more you talk to cats, he believed, the smarter they become.

Immediately they remembered the back porch with its concrete floor warmed by the sun's rays. They rushed out to curl and uncurl on its rough surface. Then Koko stretched out to his full length, the better to absorb warmth in every glistening cat hair.

Qwilleran thought, *He loves the sun, and the sun loves him.* He was quoting another journalist, Christopher Smart, who had written a poem about his cat Jeoffrey. It was rich in quotable lines, even though Christopher and Jeoffrey had lived in the eighteenth century.

While the Siamese lounged al fresco, Qwilleran unpacked the van—first, the recumbent bicycle. The tough old trail bike was in the toolshed, but the snooty technological freak with basket seat and elevated pedals deserved more respect. He parked it on the kitchen porch. Trial runs on the backroads of Pickax had convinced him that it was safer, speedier, and less tiring than conventional bikes. Whether he would have the nerve to ride such a curiosity in tradition-bound Mooseville was yet to be decided.

Other baggage from the van made itself at home: clothing in the sleeping cubicle, writing materials in the office cubicle, books on shelves in the main room. Two exceptions went on the coffee table: the Thomas Hardy novel because of its impressive leather binding, and *Mark Twain A to Z* because of its large size. Koko liked to sit on large books.

There was a second screened porch on the lakeside—with a magnificent view and plenty of afternoon sun—but the concrete floor was not good for rolling, the Siamese had discovered. Sand tracked in from the beach or was blown in by prevailing winds.

The cabin perched on a lofty sand dune that had been hundreds of years in the making, its steep slope anchored by beach grass and milkweed. A sandladder led down to the beach; it was simply a framework of two-by-fours filled in with loose sand for treads.

Qwilleran, dressed for dinner in white shorts and black polo shirt, stood at the top of the sandladder, and noticed that the beach had changed. Normally an expanse of deep, dry sand, it was now a hard, flat pebbly surface, while the loose sand had

blown up into a ridge at the foot of the
dune. It might blow away or wash away in
the next storm; that was the fascination of
living at the shore. The water itself could
change from calm to turbulent in five minutes, while its color shifted from blue to
turquoise to green.

He walked along the shore to the Rikers' beach house. The first half-mile bordered his own property and included the
stony Seagull Point. Then came the row of
cottages known as Top o' the Dune Club.
This year they had been given names, displayed on rustic signs of routed wood. The
golfing Mableys called their place THE SAND
TRAP. The old Dunfield cottage, said to be
haunted, was now LITTLE MANDERLEY. A little frame house called THE LITTLE FRAME
HOUSE was understandable when one
knew the owners had a picture-framing
business. Then there was BAH HUMBUG,
which could belong only to the Comptons;
Lyle was superintendent of schools, a
grouch with a sense of humor.

Most of the cottagers were on their
decks, and they waved at Qwilleran; some
invited him up for a drink.

Last in the row was the Rikers' cottage, a yellow frame bungalow called SUNNY DAZE.

"Is that the cleverest name you could think of?" Qwilleran asked Arch, never missing a chance to needle his old friend. Arch was serving drinks; Mildred was serving canapés. The Comptons were there, and Toulouse sat on the deck railing—a silent bundle of black-and-white fur.

"Does he ever say anything?" Qwilleran asked, comparing his silence with Koko's electronic yowl.

"He says a polite meow when I feed him," Mildred said. "For a stray he's very well-mannered."

She was wearing a caftan intended to disguise her plumpness. Her husband's leisure garb did nothing to camouflage his well-fed silhouette, but he was happy and relaxed. By comparison, the superintendent of schools looked underfed and overworked after three decades of coping with school boards, teachers, and parents. Lisa Compton was as pleasant as her husband pretended to be grouchy.

Mildred announced, "Qwill has built a guest house!"

"Expecting a lot of company?" Lisa asked.

"No, it's strictly for emergency overnights," he said. "It's a little larger than a dollhouse and a little more comfortable than a tent. I come up here to get away from it all and don't encourage guests."

Lisa asked about Polly Duncan; they were usually seen together at dinner parties.

"She's traveling in Canada with her sister during July."

"A whole month? You'll miss her," Mildred said.

He shrugged. "She went to England for a whole summer, and I survived." The truth was: already he missed their nightly phone calls, and he would miss their weekends even more. "Has anyone tried the new restaurant?"

No one had, but they had read about it on the food page of the *Something*. A couple had come from Florida to run it during the summer months; the wife was the chef, with a bachelor's degree from a culinary institute. It sounded promising.

Mildred said, "We stressed her training because MCCC will soon have a chef's school, and we knew our readers would be curious about the curriculum in a school like that. It was a generous feature, but the chef's husband had the bad taste to phone and complain because we didn't price the entrées or list the desserts."

Lisa nodded wisely. "He was jealous because his wife got all the attention, and he wasn't even in the photo."

Then they discussed the backpacker mystery (no conclusion) . . . the Sand Giant's Gnomes (nice kids) . . . the sudden naming of beach houses (someone's nephew was in the sign business).

Qwilleran asked Lyle, "What's new in the school system? Any conspiracies? Any bloodshed?"

"I'll tell you what's happening," Lyle said crisply. "The K Fund has been so generous with our schools that we've gone from the lowest per-student expenditure to the highest in the state! So our share of state funding has been reduced to peanuts. At the same time—they're telling us *what and how to teach*!"

"And if we don't comply," Lisa put in, "they're threatening to take over our schools!"

"Over my dead body!" Lyle said. "Our school system will go private! The whole county will secede from the state: the Principality of Moose, 400 miles north of everywhere, with our own government, our own tax laws, our own education system!"

"And my husband as reigning monarch," Lisa cried. "King Lyle the First!"

"Thank you," he said. "Qwill can be chancellor of the exchequer, and Arch can be master of the royal cellar."

"I'll drink to that," said the host as he uncorked another bottle.

While he served, Lisa asked Qwilleran about his vacation plans, and Lyle asked if he had brought his weird bicycle.

"If you refer to the recumbent . . . yes, I brought it, but I plan to ride only on back roads. Mooseville isn't ready for state-of-the-art technology."

"And what do you intend to read?" Mildred asked.

"Chiefly old editions of Mark Twain that Eddington Smith has found in estate sales. It's amazing how bookish previous generations were in this remote corner of the country."

"There was no electronic entertainment," Lyle said. "Also, there was a lot of affluence in the nineteenth century, and an impressive library gave the family status, whether or not they read the books— probably not. I imagine you run across many uncut pages, Qwill."

"Yes, but not in Mark Twain's books; they're all well thumbed."

"He came through here on a lecture tour," Lisa said. "My great-grandmother had a crush on him. She fell for his moustache. I have her diary. The pages are brown, and the ink is fading, but it's full of fascinating stuff."

Qwilleran made a mental note for the "Qwill Pen": Lisa Compton's great-grandmother's diary.

When Mildred invited them indoors to the table and they were spooning butternut and roasted pepper soup, she asked, "Is everyone going to the Fryers Club play? It may be Fran Brodie's last production. I hear she's had a good job offer in Chicago. She was there for two weeks, working on the hotel do-over."

"Bad news!" Lisa moaned. "What can we do to keep her here?"

"Get Dr. Prelligate to propose marriage. They've been seeing a lot of each other."

Arch said, "It'll take more than a college president to keep Fran down on the farm. Get Qwilleran to propose . . ."

"Arch, honey, would you pour the wine? I'm ready to serve the chops," Mildred interrupted.

With the coddled chops were twice-baked potatoes, a broccoli soufflé, a pinot noir, and a toast from Lyle Compton: "Thursday's Independence Day! Let's drink to the genius who single-handedly dragged the Fourth of July parade from the pits and launched it to the stars!"

"Hear! Hear!" the others shouted with vigor.

Mildred blushed. "Lyle, I didn't know you could be so poetic!"

"Speech! Speech!"

"Well, our parades were getting to be all commercial and political. The last straw was a candy-grabbing free-for-all for kids, with rock music blaring from a sound truck, and not an American flag in sight! Someone had to put a foot down, and I have big feet!"

"That's my wife," Arch said proudly.

"This year's parade will have flags, marching bands, floats, grass-roots participation, and a little originality. Athletes from Mooseland High, wearing their uniforms, will march in four rows of five each, carrying banners with a single letter of the alphabet. Each row will spell a word: PEACE, TRUTH, HONOR, and TRUST."

"Very clever," said Lisa. "Who's the grand marshal?"

"Andrew Brodie, in Scottish regalia, with his bagpipe. He'll march just ahead of the color guard and play patriotic tunes in slow tempo."

"Maybe it's because I was born a Campbell," Lisa said, "but there's something about bagpipe music that makes me limp with emotion."

"The floats will be sponsored by the chamber of commerce, parent-teachers, commercial fisheries, private marinas, and the Friends of Wool." Mildred referred to a new coalition of wool-growers, spinners, knitters, and other fiber artists. "Barb Ogilvie is our mentor—very talented. She teaches knitting, started the knitting club, and runs a knitting day camp for kids. In high school she was considered a bit wild, but she's settled down. Did Arch tell you he's learning to knit socks?"

Qwilleran turned to his lifelong friend in astonishment. "Arch! Why were you keeping this dirty little secret from me?"

"What the heck! It's one of the things you do when you're middle-aged and in love."

"Lyle never says sweet things like that," Lisa complained.

There was a moment of silence, which Qwilleran interrupted by asking, "What are the Friends of Wool going to do on a float?"

"We'll have live sheep, a shepherd playing a flute, two spinners spinning, and six knitters knitting—four women and two men, if Arch will consent. Dr. Emerson, the surgeon, has agreed, and I think it would add prestige if the publisher of the newspaper were on the float, knitting a sock with four needles."

As all eyes turned to him, he said, "To quote Shakespeare: I don't wanna, I don't hafta, and I ain't gonna."

His wife smiled knowingly at the others.

After an old-fashioned Waldorf salad, and Black Forest cake, and coffee, Lyle wanted to smoke a cigar, and the other two men accompanied him down the sandladder to the beach.

Their first comment was about the miniature sand dune recently formed. It extended at least a mile to everyone's knowledge.

"Some day," Lyle predicted, "it will be thirty feet high, and our cottages will have crumbled to dust, leaving only the stone chimneys. Tour groups from other planets will gawk at these monuments as tour guides explain that they had religious significance, being used to ensure fertility and ward off famine."

Qwilleran skipped a few stones across the placid lake surface.

"You're good at that," Arch said. "That's something I could never learn to do."

"It's one of my few talents. I could never learn to knit a sock."

Lyle said, "You should ride on the float, Arch. I'm going to be on the PTA float. We're reproducing a one-room school with old desks and blackboards, a pot-bellied stove, and everyone in nineteenth-century costume. I'm going to be the principal in a frock coat and pince-nez eyeglasses, brandishing a whipping cane. I expect to get booed by the parade-watchers. I just hope they don't throw eggs."

He finished his cigar, and they climbed the sandladder to the deck, where the two women were giggling suspiciously.

Mildred said, "Qwill, I'd like to ask you a great favor."

"It would be a privilege and a pleasure." He could never say no to Mildred; she was so sincere, generous, and good-natured, and she was such a good cook.

"Well, the parade opens with a 1776 tableau on a float—the signing of the Declaration of Independence—and it ends with a flock of bicycles: Wouldn't it be a terrific finale if you brought up the rear with your high-tech recumbent bike?"

Qwilleran hesitated only a second. "I'm not too enthusiastic about the idea, but . . . I'll pedal with my feet up in the air . . . if Arch will ride on your float, knitting a sock."

3

Ordinarily, Koko was a feline alarm clock at eleven P.M., reminding the world at large that it was time for a bedtime snack and lights-out, so his behavior on his first night at the cabin made Qwilleran wonder. The three of them had been lolling on the screened porch in the dark, watching the fireflies blink their little flashlights. The porch was furnished with cushioned chairs and a dining set in weatherproof molded resin—white at Fran Brodie's suggestion, as a foil for the dark logs. While Qwilleran and Yum Yum enjoyed the luxury of cushions, Koko huddled on the dining table, perhaps because it gave him an elevated view of the dark beachfront.

Eventually Yum Yum became restless, leading Qwilleran to consult his watch and announce "Treat!" She scampered after him when he went indoors to serve the Kabibbles, but Koko stayed where he was. Something's down there, Qwilleran realized—something I can't see. It was a clear night, the stars were bright, the crickets were chirping, somewhere an owl was hooting, and a gentle surf splashed rhythmically on the shore. It was a pleasant night, too, with no chill in the air, so Qwilleran left the door to the porch open when he retired to his sleeping cubicle. Koko could come indoors if the scene became boring; he could join Yum Yum on the blue cushion atop the refrigerator.

Qwilleran had a dream that night. He always dreamed after eating pork. In his dream, Moose County had seceded from the state and was an independent principality ruled by a royal family, prime minister, cabinet, and national council—but they were all cats! There was nothing original about the scenario; he had been reading *A Connecticut Yankee in King Arthur's Court*, in which a character suggested feline rule as an improvement over the existing system. In Qwilleran's dream, the royal cat family was shown to be intelligent, entertaining, and inexpensive to maintain. He was sorry to wake up.

He found Koko none the worse for his nocturnal escapade. He ate a good breakfast and then wanted to go for a ride on Qwilleran's shoulder. He kept jumping at the latch on the screened door of the porch.

"Not now," Qwilleran told him. "Later! You've had your breakfast, and now I'm entitled to mine. This is a democratic family. You're not the ruling monarch."

Before setting off for Mooseville in his van, Qwilleran inspected his new guest accommodation. First he had to find it, hidden in the woods—the same size as the toolshed and built of the same green-stained cedar. But the Snuggery had windows, and indoor plumbing. Modular furniture, including a double-deck bunk, made the utmost use of every inch of space. Red blankets, a red rug, and a framed picture of poppies were a trifle overpowering in the small quarters—but cheerful. Qwilleran thought, It's not a bad place to stay overnight, but I wouldn't want to stay two nights. Fran knew what she was doing.

From there he drove along the lakeshore to Mooseville, a quaint resort town two miles long and hardly more than a block wide. It was squeezed between the lake and a high wall of sand called the Great Dune. On the lake side of Main Street were the municipal docks, private marinas, bait shops, and the Northern Lights Hotel; on the other side: the bank, post office, hardware store, Shipwreck Tavern, and so on. A few side streets with names like Oak, Pine, and Maple dead-ended at the foot of the Great Dune and were lined with shops, offices, small eateries, and the Shipwreck Museum.

The Great Dune, which had taken an estimated ten thousand years to form, was held in reverence in Mooseville. It rose abruptly and towered protectively over the downtown area, crowned with a lush forest of trees. There were no structures up there. Even if building were permitted, who would dare? The sheer drop of about a hundred feet was formidable—and famous; it could be seen for miles out in the lake.

Only one thoroughfare sliced through the Great Dune, and that was Sandpit Road at the east end of downtown. It was a reminder that sand had once been mined and exported to bolster the country's failing economy. A chunk of the Great Dune had been shipped Down Below for the construction of concrete highways, bridges, and skyscrapers—like a little bit of Moose County in cities all over the northeast central United States.

On the first day of Qwilleran's vacation he always made the rounds, renewing his acquaintance with business people—asking about their winter doings and summer prospects. It was neighborly, and also good public relations for the newspaper. On this morning he had breakfast at the hotel and shook hands with the owners. He shook hands with the bank manager and cashed a check. He shook hands with the postmaster and told her he expected to receive mail addressed to General Delivery; three postcards had already arrived.

At Grott's Grocery he shook hands with the whole family and bought some boiled ham for sandwiches. He shook hands with the druggist and stocked up on hard and soft beverages for possible guests.

At the Shipwreck Tavern he shook hands with the bartender. "Still drinkin' Squunk water?" the man asked. "Have one on the house."

"I believe in supporting local products," Qwilleran said. It was a mineral water from a spring in Squunk Corners. "Expecting a lot of business tomorrow?"

"Nah. Parades are family days. Not much serious drinkin'."

"Any developments in the case of the missing backpacker?"

"Nah. I say it's a lot of hokum, like the two-headed raccoon a coupla years back. Gives folks somethin' to talk about."

Next, Qwilleran went to Huggins Hardware for mosquito repellent and shook hands with Cecil Huggins and his great-uncle, a white-bearded man who had worked in the store since the age of twelve.

"Mosquitoes not so bad this year, are they, Unc?"

"Nope," said the old man. "Weather's too dry."

The store had a carefully cultivated old-time country-store atmosphere that appealed to vacationers from Down Below: rough wood floors, old showcases, and such merchandise as pitchforks, kerosene lanterns, fifty-pound salt blocks, goat feed, and nails by the pound.

"What can you tell me about the new restaurant?" Qwilleran asked.

"On Sandpit Road, across from the Great Dune Motel," Cecil replied. "Same building where the Chinese restaurant opened and closed last summer. A couple came up from Florida to run it for the tourist season. The chamber of commerce ran an ad in Florida papers—business opportunity with special perks. The guy's name is Owen Bowen. His wife's the chef."

"Food's too fancy," said the old man.

"Perhaps for campers and locals," Cecil admitted, "but the whole idea is to get summer people from the Grand Island Club to come here on their yachts and spend money."

"What were the special perks?"

"Pretty generous, we thought. The landlord gave him a break on the rent. The Northern Lights Hotel gave him a suite for the price of a single. Chamber members pitched in and redecorated the restaurant before the Bowens got here."

"'T were all red last year," said Unc.

"Yes, we painted the walls, cleaned the kitchen, washed the windows . . . You'd think he'd be tickled pink, wouldn't you? But no! He came to a chamber meeting bellyaching about this, that, and the other thing. Then he wanted us to change the name of the Great Dune to the White Cliffs. He said it was more glamorous, more promotable. He talked down to us as if we were a bunch of hicks."

"And how did that suggestion go over?" Qwilleran asked.

"Like a lead balloon! Everybody knows a cliff is rock. Our dune is pure sand. Cliffs are a dime a dozen, but where can you find a dune like ours? We voted against the idea unanimously, and he stomped out of the meeting like a spoiled kid."

"If he ain't careful," the old man said with a chuckle, "he'll get the Sand Giant riled up."

Qwilleran said he hoped the food was

better than Owen's personality. "Have you tried it?"

"Not yet, but they say it's good. They say his wife's nice. Too bad Owen turned out to be disagreeable."

"He's a horse's tail!" said Unc.

"One more thing," Qwilleran mentioned. "I have a screened door with a rat-tail latch that gets stuck. The bar doesn't drop. I'm afraid the cats could push the door open."

"Easy," said Cecil and sold him a can of spray-lubricant.

After the formal hand-shaking, Qwilleran ambled over to Elizabeth Hart's boutique on Oak Street at the foot of the Great Dune. Having saved her life once upon a time he felt a godfatherly interest in her well-being. She had belonged to the Grand Island set, and there was something subtly different in her grooming, clothing, speech, manner, and ideas. A Chicago heiress, she had visited Moose County, met Derek Cuttlebrink, and decided to stay. They were good for each other. He had toned down her citified pretensions without spoiling her individuality; she had convinced him to enroll in restaurant management at Moose County Community College, and it was Derek who had renamed her boutique.

It was now called Elizabeth's Magic. Unlike the surrounding souvenir shops, it featured exotic wearables, crafts by local artisans, and such mystic paraphernalia as tarot cards, rune stones, Ouija boards, and good-luck jewelry. There was also a coffee dispenser in the rear of the shop and a ring of chairs in aluminum and black nylon.

When Qwilleran walked in, Elizabeth was busy with customers but waved an airy greeting and said, "Don't go away; I have news for you." For a few minutes he joined the browsers, then gravitated toward the coffee dispensary. After a while, Elizabeth joined him, leaving a husky male assistant to keep an eye on idle sightseers and take the money of paying customers.

Qwilleran asked, "Is your shop sponsoring a football team? Or is he a bouncer?" He was one of the big blond youths indigenous to the north country.

"That's Kenneth, a rising senior at Mooseland High," she said. "He's my stockboy and delivery man, and I'm breaking him in on sales ... Are you going to the parade tomorrow, Qwill? I designed the chamber of commerce float—the signing of the Declaration of Independence, based on the John Turnbull painting."

"I know it," Qwilleran said. "It's in Philadelphia. Who'll play the roles of the signers?"

"C of C members, all in 1776 costumes: wigs, knee breeches, satin waistcoats, jabots, buckle shoes. We're renting everything from a theater supply house in Chicago."

"That's a big investment," Qwilleran said. "Who's paying?"

"You!" she said with glee. "Well, not exactly you, but the K Fund. We applied for a grant."

"Is Derek going to be in the parade?"

"No. The play at the barn opens Friday, and he has the title role. He's concentrating on that. But the big news is that he has a job! Assistant manager at the new restaurant. They have a sophisticated menu and a good wine list, so he hopes he'll learn something."

"Have you met Owen Bowen?"

"Only at a C of C meeting. He's middle-aged, quite handsome, rather supercil-

ious, and *ever so tan*," she said disdain-
fully. "I consider him a bit of a pill, but
Derek can handle him."

"I believe it." Derek's height (six-feet-
eight) coupled with his swaggering but lik-
able personality appealed to young girls,
bosses, grandmothers, and cats and dogs.

Elizabeth said, "It was Derek who
named the new restaurant. The psychology of naming food establishments is
something he learned at MCCC. Mr.
Bowen planned to name it—ugh!—the
Cliffside Café! Derek told him it was too ordinary. 'Owen's Place' has an element of
played-down snob appeal that will attract
the yachting crowd from Grand Island."

At this point she was called to the front
of the store, and Qwilleran looked at a sailboat in the craft display. It was handcrafted
entirely of copper—labeled "Sloop rigged
with topsail, mainsail, jib sail, and spin-
naker—by Mile Zander." He was a commercial fisherman whose hobby was
metalwork.

"Does the pedestal go with it?"
Qwilleran asked Kenneth.

"I dunno, but the guy'd sell it to you, I

bet. It weighs a ton. I'll deliver it if you want."

When Qwilleran drove away, he had bought a copper sculpture and a railroad tie. He had always liked sailboats, although he had never learned the difference between a sloop, a yawl, and a ketch. He bought yachting magazines and read about the cup races, and the sight of a sailboat regatta breezing along the horizon quickened his pulse. Now he could tell Arch he had bought a sailboat and would watch his old friend's jaw drop.

Before going home, he drove out to Fishport to see Doris Hawley—for several reasons.

Beyond the Mooseville town limits he passed a former canning factory that had once supplied half the nation with smoked herring; now it housed an animal clinic, a video store, and a coin-operated laundry . . . Farther along the highway the FOO restaurant had not yet replaced the letter D that blew off its sign in a northern hurricane two decades ago . . . Next came the fisheries, a complex of weathered sheds and wharves; they were silent as death when the fleet was out but a scene of manic activity when the catch came in . . . Beyond the Roaring Creek bridge, on the left, was the trailer home of Magnus and Doris Hawley. A homemade sign on the lawn—a square of plywood nailed to a post—said   HOME-BAKES.   That   meant muffins, cinnamon rolls, and cookies. Mrs. Hawley was watering the extensive flower garden when Qwilleran pulled into the side drive.

"Beautiful garden, Mrs. Hawley!" he called out. "You must have two green thumbs!"

"Oh, hello, Mr. Q." She turned off the spray and dropped the nozzle. "It's been awfully dry. Don't know when I saw such a stretch without rain. What can I do for you?"

"Do you happen to have any cinnamon rolls?"

"Half-pan or whole pan? They freeze nicely . . . Hush!" she said to a barking ter-rier, who ran excitedly back and forth on his trolley. She was a gray-haired woman with a gardener's slight stoop and the en-ergy of a much younger person.

When   she   went   into   the   house,

Qwilleran looked toward the rear of the property and saw a picnic bench on a grassy bank, but the dry spell had tamed the Roaring Creek to a gurgle. "Is Magnus working the boats today?" he asked when she returned.

"Oh, you can't keep that man off the boats!" she said with pride as well as disapproval. "He's seventy and could retire, but what would he do? Winters are bad enough. He does a little ice-fishing but watches an awful lot of television."

"And how do you cope with a Fishport winter?"

"Well, I don't have any garden or any customers for home-bakes, so I read books and write letters to our sons Down Below."

"If you don't mind a suggestion," Qwilleran said, "why don't you get into the literacy program and teach adults how to read? Pickax has an active program, and I imagine this community could use one."

Mrs. Hawley was aghast. "I wouldn't know how to do that! I don't think I could!"

"They'd give you a training course in tutoring. Think it over. Meanwhile, have you heard anything about the young man you befriended?"

"Not a thing! The police were here twice, asking questions. We've told them everything we know! They act as if we're holding something back. It makes me nervous. And some nasty people are saying my cookies were poisoned. I haven't sold a one since that rumor started. I worry about the whole thing."

"You have nothing to worry about, Mrs. Hawley. The nasty people will choke on their own lies. As for the police, they're trained to investigate in certain ways. I'm sorry your act of kindness boomeranged."

"You're very kind, Mr. Q. I'll tell Magnus what you said."

"By the way, do you know someone named Mike Zander?"

"Why, yes! He's on the boats. They go to our church. His wife just had a beautiful baby boy."

"Did you know he's quite an artist? I've purchased one of his sculptures."

"That's nice. They can use the money. I'd heard that he putters around with metal in his spare time. Are you going to the parade tomorrow, Mr. Q? Magnus will be on the float sponsored by the fisheries. I can't tell you anything about it, because it's kind of a secret joke."

"Those fishermen are great jokers when they get their heads together," Qwilleran said.

"Four generations of our family will be on the sidelines, including my widowed mother-in-law, who's a great fan of yours, Mr. Q. She's embroidering a sampler for you!"

"That's thoughtful of her." He mustered as much enthusiasm as he could. "What's a sampler?"

"A motto that you can frame and hang on the wall."

Devoted readers liked to send him useless knickknacks made by their own loving hands, and it was to his credit that he always sent a hand-written thank-you. During his boyhood, he had written countless thank-you letters to his mother's friends who sent him toys and books that were three years too young for him. His mother always said, "Jamie, we accept gifts in the spirit in which they were given."

To Mrs. Hawley he said, "Well, well! A sampler! That's something to look forward to, isn't it?"

Driving home, Qwilleran wondered what a fisherman's widow would choose to embroider for him. *Home Sweet Home*? *Love One Another*? He had seen these words of wisdom in antique shops, worked with thousands of stitches and framed in tarnished gilt. He had never seen *Slide, Kelly, Slide* or *Nice Guys Finish Last,* or his mother's favorite maxim: *Keep Your Eye Upon the Doughnut and Not Upon the Hole*. Growing up in a one-parent household, he had heard that advice a thousand times. Instead of turning him into an optimist, however, it had made him a doughnut addict. What he really liked was the traditional fried-cake with cake-like texture and crisp brown crust redolent of hot cooking oil.

As he drove he watched automatically for the old schoolhouse chimney, then turned left into the long K driveway. Halfway up the twisting dirt lane he could hear Koko yowling; the cat knew he was coming. The noisy welcome could mean that the phone had been ringing, or something had been knocked down and smashed, or the radio had been left on, or there was a plumbing leak.

"Cool it, old boy. Nothing's wrong," Qwilleran said after inspecting the premises, but Koko continued to frisk about. When he jumped up at the peg where his harness hung, the message was clear: He wanted to go for a walk. Qwilleran obliged—and recorded the cat's antics in his personal journal. It was not a real diary—just a spiral notebook in which he described noteworthy moments in his life. This was one of them. The report was headed "Mooseville, Wednesday, July 3."

Koko did it again! He solved a mystery that was boggling the gossips around here. Nobody but me will ever know. If the media discovered this cat's psychic tendencies, they'd give us no peace.

What happened, Koko wanted to go for a walk on the beach, meaning that I walk and he rides—on my shoulder. That way, he doesn't bog down in deep sand or cut his precious toes on sharp pebbles. Smart cat! He wears a harness, and I keep a firm hand on the leash.

All day long he'd wanted to explore the beach. Finally we buckled up and went down the sandladder. I started to walk west toward town, but Koko made a royal ruckus; he wanted to go east. Toward Seagull Point, I imagined. But we hadn't gone far before a strange growl came from the cat's innards, and his body stiffened. Then, impulsively, he wanted to get down on the sand. Keeping a taut leash, I let him go.

Well, to watch him struggle through that deep sand would have been comic if it weren't that he was dead serious. When he reached the sand ridge, he climbed up the slope, slipping and sliding. I was tempted to give him a boost but didn't. This whole expedition was his idea.

By the time he reached the top he was really growling, and he started to dig. Sand flew! But most of it trickled back into the excavation. Koko wouldn't give up, though. What was he after? A dead seagull buried in the sand? He dug and he dug, and I started to get suspicious.

"Look out!" I said, pushing him aside. I saw something shining in the hole. The sun was hitting something that glinted. It was the face of a wristwatch! I grabbed Koko and ran back to the cabin.

After calling 911, Qwilleran gave Koko a treat. There was not long to wait. The sheriff's department knew the K cabin; they checked it regularly during the winter. In a matter of minutes a patrol car came through the woods, and a deputy in a wide-brimmed hat stepped out. Qwilleran went out to meet her—Moose County's first woman deputy.

"You reported finding a body?" she asked impassively.

"Down on the beach, buried in the sand. I'll show you the way."

She followed him down the sandladder and along the shore to Koko's excavation. "How'd you find it?"

"Just walking on the beach."

She examined the hole. "Looks like some animal's been digging."

"It seems so, doesn't it?"

Unhooking her phone, she called the

state police post, and Qwilleran said he would go back to the cabin and direct whoever responded.

In the next half-hour the clearing filled with vehicles. Qwilleran met each one and pointed to the sandladder; otherwise, he stayed out of sight:

First, the state police car with two officers.

Second, the ambulance of the rescue squad. They had shovels and a stretcher.

Then, another sheriff's car with two passengers in the backseat. Magnus and Doris Hawley were escorted down the sandladder by the deputy.

Soon, the helicopter from Pickax, landing on the hard flat sand near the water. That would be the medical examiner, Qwilleran presumed.

Unexpectedly, a blue pickup delivering the railroad tie and copper sculpture. "Hey, what's goin' on here?" Kenneth asked.

"A simulated rescue drill. My responsibility is to keep the driveway open. So just drop the stuff and go back down the drive."

"Hey, this is cool! How old is this cabin?"

"I don't know," Qwilleran said. "I'll take the sculpture. You take the tie around to the lakeside and put it on the screened porch. I'll lead the way."

With some prodding, Kenneth positioned the tie in the northwest corner of the porch. "Hey, some view you got here!"

"Yes. This way out . . ."

"Are those . . . cats?"

"Yes. Come on, Kenneth. This drill is being timed to the split second . . . On the double!"

Qwilleran packed him off down the driveway, just as the deputy escorted the Hawleys up the sandladder. Qwilleran ducked indoors. They drove away. Then the ambulance left. The helicopter lifted off, taking a blue body bag on a stretcher. When the state troopers drove away, only Deputy Greenleaf remained, and Qwilleran went out to size her up. Though not bad looking, she was stony-faced, a mask that seemed to go with the wide-brimmed hats worn by deputies.

Glancing at him and getting out her pad, she said, "You must be Mr. Q."

"Yes, but are you aware of the department's policy?"

"We don't release your name."

"That's right. You must be Deputy Greenleaf." It had said in the paper that a woman deputy was needed to escort women prisoners to the Bixby County detention facility. "Glad to have you in the department."

She nodded, and the tassels on her hat bobbed.

Now Qwilleran knew why Koko had stayed up all night; he knew what was on the beach. If he had not campaigned for an outing on the shore . . . if he had not insisted on going east instead of west . . . if he had not started digging at one particular spot, the backpacker mystery would remain unsolved. Most cats had a sixth sense, but Koko's perception of right and wrong went beyond catly concerns. He sensed answers to the questions that baffled humans and found ways of communicating his findings. Qwilleran could attribute his talents only to his magnificent whiskers. Yum Yum had the standard forty-eight; Koko had sixty.

Qwilleran had reasons for being secretive about Koko's special gifts and his own involvement, and he was relieved to hear the six o'clock newscast on WPKX: "Acting on a tip from a beachcomber, the sheriff's department today found the body of the backpacker missing since Friday. It was buried in the sand near Mooseville. The deceased was identified by Magnus and Doris Hawley as the hiker who had come to their house asking permission to camp on their property. Cause of death has not been determined, according to a sheriff's spokesperson. Identification was found on the body but is being withheld pending notification of family. The deceased was not from the tri-county area."

The locals always felt better when the subject of an accident or crime was not one of their own.

Arch Riker would be furious, Qwilleran knew, because the newsbreak had happened on the radio station's time, and the *Something* could not cover it until Friday; no paper was published on the holiday.

Qwilleran himself was pleased with the way things had turned out and proposed to reward the Siamese with a session of reading aloud. They always enjoyed the sound of his voice, and he rather enjoyed it, too. He suggested *Far from the Madding Crowd*. "You'll like it," he said. "It's about sheep and cows. There's also a dog named George and a cat who plays a minor role."

His readings for the Siamese were always dramatized by sound effects. His theater training in college had made him an expert at bleating, barking, and meowing—if nothing else—and the cats especially liked the lowing of cattle. He did a two-note "moo-oo" like a foghorn. When he mooed, they looked at him with a do-it-again expression in their alert blue eyes, and he did it again. To tell the truth, he enjoyed mooing.

After the reading, he unpacked the sailboat that Kenneth had delivered. Yum Yum assisted. She had a vested interest in shiny objects, cardboard boxes, and crumpled paper, and the carton was stuffed with crumpled sheets of the *Moose County Something*.

The sailboat looked larger than it had in the store among all the other merchandise. A foot tall, it was constructed of sheet copper that had been treated to retain color and brilliance, and it was dazzling in the light from the skywindows. The sails, tilted at realistic angles, played with the light and gave added dimension to the sculpture. To stabilize the lightweight object, there was a heavy base of wood, chipped to suggest choppy water, with the keel cemented into a groove. It was a clever and eye-catching piece of work.

Qwilleran carried it to the porch, only to discover that Koko had taken possession of the pedestal, where he posed like an ancient Egyptian cat.

"Jump down," Qwilleran said foolishly, knowing that Koko never jumped down when told to jump down. So he left the sailboat on the table and went to write some more in his journal.

He had long wanted to keep a journal; some day he might want to write a memoir. He should have started at an early age, but he had always been too busy growing up, playing baseball, acting in plays, sowing wild oats, discovering the work ethic, hanging around press clubs, and making life-threatening mistakes. Now at last he was a journalist with a personal journal.

4

The Fourth of July parade was scheduled
to start at one P.M., and Qwilleran reported
early to scout around. Never having partic-
ipated in a parade, he was curious about
the preparations behind the scene. He
thought it must be a masterpiece of orga-
nization, and it was!

The staging area was beyond the town
limits, with parade units assigned to spe-
cific parking lots or open fields. Marchers
were close to the starting point, and mech-
anized units were farthest away; that made
sense. In between, assigned to the parking

lot of the FOO restaurant, were the bikers. They were a colorful troupe. Qwilleran himself wore white shorts, a blue-and-white-striped T-shirt, and a red baseball cap. There were trail bikes, school bikes, plenty of racers, and one old-fashioned high-wheeler. He left his recumbent locked in his van and went exploring with a camera hanging about his neck.

The floats interested him most. There were five lined up on the highway— flatbeds skirted with tricolor bunting and identifying banners: "Signing of the Declaration of Independence," "Dear Old Golden Schooldays," "Friends of Wool." A twenty-four-foot sailboat on a dolly, called *Smooth Sailing*, was sponsored jointly by the private marinas, its sails furled and its deck awash with young persons in skimpy swimwear. The fifth float was the one Mrs. Hawley had mentioned. It was called "Feedin' the Chickens." Three commercial fishermen in slickers, boots, and rubber gloves were laughing and clowning as they waited for the signal to move. On the flatbed were a couple of barrels, a weathered table, and stacks of wooden boxes.

Qwilleran signaled to Magnus Hawley, one of the three. "Explain the name of your float," he asked.

"Well, see, soon's we get rollin', we start dressin' the fish in the boxes and throwin' the guts and heads in the gut barrels. That's when the gulls come out from nowhere. Chickens, we call 'em. First two or three, then a whole flock, followin' us down the whole route, catchin' the heads before they hit the barrel. By the time we get to the end, there'll be a hunerd!" He roared with laughter. "Some show!"

As parade time drew near, the official starter in his tricolor top hat ran up and down the highway, waving his arms and yelling. His aides in tricolor sashes and baseball caps checked the individual units. Standing by was the sheriff's car that would precede the parade at four miles an hour to clear the road and order watchers back onto the sidewalks; Deputy Greenleaf was at the wheel. The color guard stood solemnly at parade-rest—the flag-bearers flanked by members of the military, rifles by their sides.

Highly visible was Andrew Brodie, the Pickax police chief. As grand marshal, the Scots bagpiper would lead the parade in full Highland regalia. He was a big man in any uniform but a giant when swaggering in his lofty feather "bonnet" with a shoulderful of plaid and an armful of pipes.

There was an air of frenzy around the marching units, however. Besides the two bands there were three restless groups: the Parade of Pets, Parade of Moms, and Athletes for Peace. To add to the confusion, the high school band was practicing—no two musicians playing the same number—while the middle-schoolers in the fife-and-drum corps were warming up and had reached fever pitch. Nervous parents were cautioning children who would trudge the course with cats and dogs on leashes or in wagons. Moms were trying to quiet their youngest, who would ride in strollers, baby buggies, backpacks, or even wheelbarrows.

As for the Athletes for Peace, their staging area was a madhouse. Young persons, each with a large letter of the alphabet on a pole, were running around in a state of hysteria, shouting and laughing like maniacs. They had discovered they could scramble their letters to spell CHEAT, SHOOT, TREASON, and worse! The coach in charge of the unit blew his whistle and yelled at deaf ears.

The official starter was frantic. The sheriff's car, the grand marshal, and the color guard were lined up. The first float was pulling up with its serious statesmen in wigs and knee breeches, but the athletes were out of control. "What do we do?" the starter cried to his aides. "Do we cancel 'em?"

At that moment, two gunshots sounded above the din. The effect was paralyzing. Everything stopped. No one moved. The silence was heavy with unasked questions.

Then the coach blew his whistle. "Fall in!"

The sheriff's car started to roll. After giving it a fifty-yard head start, the piper began his slow, swinging gait and skirling rendition of the national anthem. The color guard snapped to attention.

No one asked who had fired the shots, but Qwilleran had an idea.

One by one, the units moved out of the

staging area in the correct order, with floats and marchers and bands alternating appropriately.

Qwilleran, waiting for the bikers to be signaled, watched the Friends of Wool roll past. The shepherd stood knee-deep in a small flock of sheep and baby lambs and played his flute. Two spinners dressed as pioneer women sat in antique chairs and treadled their wheels. Six similar chairs were arranged back-to-back for the knitters: four women and two men.

Finally the Parade of Bikers was given the signal. The first to take off was the high-wheeler, followed by neat rows of bikes pedaled by men and women, girls and boys, in colorful helmets. Bringing up the rear was the most prominent man in the county, reclining in a bucket seat with his feet elevated. Everyone recognized the moustache, and while they applauded, cheered, screamed, and whistled, Qwilleran drew on his theater training and pedaled with unflappable cool.

The onlookers swarmed into the road and followed the recumbent—a Pied Piper with wheels. Whether their acclaim was for the bike, or the famous moustache, or the man behind the K Fund . . . that was anyone's guess.

The destaging area of the parade was the high school parking lot on the eastside, and when Qwilleran arrived, he found a traffic jam. Floats were scattered helter-skelter. Families arrived to pick up their athletes, musicians, moms, pets, and bathing beauties. Two school buses were waiting to transport float personnel back to their vehicles on the westside. A truck from the Ogilvie Sheep Ranch was collecting sheep, spinning wheels, and antique chairs.

Qwilleran grabbed Mildred's arm just as she was boarding the bus. "You got me into this. How about getting me out?"

"What's the problem, Qwill?"

He said, "I can't take my bike on the bus. You take my car keys and bring my van down here. It's a brown van—in the FOO parking lot."

She took his keys. "What did you think of our float?"

"The lambs were cute. The shepherd looked like the real thing. The sheep were fat and woolly . . . But your husband, if I may say so, looked sheepish."

"I heard that!" Arch shouted. "I wouldn't even be here if you hadn't blackmailed me, you dirty dog!"

The bus driver tooted the horn. "Come on, folks. They want us to move!"

Qwilleran had invited Andrew Brodie to stop at the cabin for a drink, following the parade, and the chief had said, "Make it at four o'clock. I've got to make an appearance at a backyard barbecue—some relatives in Black Creek."

At four o'clock, Qwilleran had a beverage tray on the porch, along with some Gorgonzola and crackers. "How was it?" he asked when his guest arrived, scowling.

"All they had to drink was iced tea! I played a tune for them and had a sandwich, then got the heck out!"

"You came to the right place, Andy. I happen to have some single-malt Scotch and good cheese."

Brodie was still in piper's garb, except for the feather bonnet and shoulder plaid. Cocked over one eye was something like a military overseas cap—in navy blue with a red pompon, cockade, and two ribbons hanging down the back. "It's a Glengarry," he said in response to Qwilleran's compliment. He tapped his left temple. "It has my clan badge."

They went out to the porch, where Koko was again on the pedestal and Yum Yum was sniffing insects on the outside of the screen. When Brodie sat down, however, she came over to inspect his brogues, bare knees, and fancy garters. Then she stood on her hind legs to see what the kilt was all about.

"She's bewildered," Qwilleran explained. "Aren't you the visitor who used to wear long pants and a shiny metal badge?"

"Where'd you get the sailboat?"

"Mike Zander made it. He's a commercial fisherman by trade."

"Sure, I know the Zanders. When I worked for the sheriff, this was my beat. Your guy must be Mike Junior. Whenever I see Mike Senior, we laugh about something that happened a few years back. It was Saturday, and the boats had just come in. Summer people were buying fish on the pier. One stuffy old biddy from Down Below looked at the fish—some of 'em still flopping around—and said in an uppity voice, 'Are you sure they're quite fresh?' The crew laughed so hard, she left in a huff."

"Those guys like a laugh," Qwilleran said. "Their chicken-feeding float had everybody running for cover!"

"We had a good day for the parade, but what we need now is some rain."

"You have to admit, though, that the dry spell has helped the mosquito situation."

"I remember one year, the town council brought in colonies of bats to get rid of mosquitoes. They scared off the tourists as well."

Qwilleran said, "Let me refresh your drink, Andy."

"I think I could stand another."

Yum Yum followed Qwilleran indoors to get a drink of water, and she looked at him so imploringly, he gave her a crumb of Gorgonzola. When he returned to the porch, Brodie was standing at the top of the sandladder.

"Your beach is a lot different this year," he said. "What's that burnt circle?"

"Some trespassers apparently had a bonfire before I got here," Qwilleran said.

"At least they didn't leave any beer cans; that's to their credit."

Brodie gave Qwilleran a sharp look. "I hear you're the one that found the body on the beach."

"Well, if you must know . . . yes." He refrained from mentioning Koko's involvement. Brodie had heard about "that smart cat" from a detective Down Below but believed only fifty percent of it—and that reluctantly. Yet both he and the prosecutor valued Qwilleran's interest in certain cases and appreciated his tips. They also respected his insistence on anonymity. Brodie, for his part, was not above leaking police information if it would aid Qwilleran's unofficial investigations. Little by little, a mutual trust had developed between the two men.

They sat in silence for a while, no doubt thinking of the same thing, until Qwilleran asked, "Were they able to identify the backpacker?"

"Oh, sure. He had an ID on his person— Philadelphia address—age twenty-five— no next of kin, but the name and phone number of a woman."

"Homicide or natural causes?"

"Homicide hasn't been ruled out . . . the coroner can't determine the cause of death. They've flown the body to the state forensic lab."

"That's strange."

"Stranger than you think. Everything points to the time of death as midnight last Friday, a few hours after he called at the Hawley house, but . . ." Brodie paused uncertainly. "There was no decomposition. Almost like he was embalmed. He'd been dead four days."

"I should cut off your drinks, Andy."

"It's the God's truth!"

"Does anyone have a theory?"

"If they do, they're not talking. The State Bureau has clamped down . . . This is all between you and me, of course."

"Of course."

"And now I've gotta take off. Thanks for the refreshments."

They walked through the cabin, Brodie looking for his Glengarry. "I thought I left it on the back of the sofa."

They looked behind the sofa cushions and in other places where he may have dropped the cap without thinking. Then Qwilleran saw Yum Yum sitting on the dining table, looking guilty. "She's attracted to small shiny objects, Andy. She pinched your clan badge! Let me look under the sofa." A few swipes with a fireplace poker produced a brown sock, a yellow pencil, and the missing cap. Qwilleran offered to brush it.

"Don't bother. I'll just give it a couple of whacks."

Qwilleran walked with him to his car, saying, "Remember the two gunshots just before the parade started? Did they ever find out who fired them?"

"Nope."

"Did they ever try?"

"Nope. It worked, didn't it? . . . how long do you plan to stay here?"

"About a month."

"We'll keep an eye on your barn."

After Brodie had driven away, Qwilleran came to a decision: Koko would never give up the railroad tie as his pedestal, his perch, his rightful eminence. The sailboat sculpture would have to go on the fireplace mantel.

Late that night the three of them sat on the porch in the dark: Koko gazing at the constellations from his private planetarium, Yum Yum fascinated by the fireflies, Qwilleran thinking his thoughts. Brodie's remark about the condition of the backpacker's body piqued his curiosity. Tomorrow he would drive to Fishport to buy some of Mrs. Hawley's home-bakes, express his relief that the fate of the young man was known, and find out how she and Magnus felt about identifying the body.

5

Friday was a gala day in Mooseville, as vacationers and locals looked forward to opening night of the barn theater. Qwilleran had promised to review the play and would first have dinner at Owen's Place; he wished Polly could be with him.

Meanwhile, he had to finish a "Qwill Pen" column and take it to the bank to be faxed before noon. He found Main Street in the throes of a holiday weekend. Throngs of vacationers sauntered along the sidewalks, looked in shop windows, licked ice cream cones, and were mesmerized by the waterfront: the lake lapping against pilings, boats gently nudging the piers, screaming seagulls catching stale bread crusts on the fly.

Next on his schedule was a drive to Fishport. What would Doris Hawley have to say about the grim task of identifying the backpacker? As soon as he crossed the Roaring Creek bridge, however, he realized it was the wrong time to ask prying questions about the condition of the corpse. Two police cars were parked in the driveway—one from the sheriff's department and the other from the state troopers' post. Furthermore, the sign on the front lawn was covered with a burlap sack, a signal that there were no baked goods for sale. He made a U-turn and returned to Mooseville.

Back in town he went into the post office and found some more postcards from Polly. He had complained, while driving her to the airport, that she never kept in touch while on vacation. She had replied, with a cryptic smile, that she would do something about it. "Doing something about it" meant mailing six cards a week— a kind of playful overkill.

In the lobby of the post office he saw a

young woman he knew, unlocking a rental box and scooping handfuls of mail into a tote bag.

"What are you doing here?" he asked. "Shouldn't you be at home?—homeschooling your brats around the kitchen table?"

She was Sharon Hanstable—plump, good-natured, and wholesomely pretty—a young version of her mother, Mildred Riker. She was also the wife of Roger MacGillivray, a reporter for the *Moose County Something*.

"I work part time at the Great Dune Motel," she explained, "and Roger's home with the kids today. He takes the weekend shift at the paper so he can have two weekdays free."

Both parents were former teachers. Sharon, after leaving that career to raise a family, was always popping up in part-time roles—as a cashier or salesclerk or short-order cook. This was an aspect of small-town life that still astounded Qwilleran.

"If you're on your way to work," he said, "I'll walk with you and carry your mail . . . Are you still enthusiastic about home-schooling?" he asked as they headed for Sandpit Road.

"It's a big job and a serious responsibility, but also a challenge and a joy," she replied. "We spend more time with our kids in positive ways. Would you like to try a session of teaching some afternoon, Qwill?"

"No, thanks. I'll take your word for it."

"Mother takes a day once in a while, so Roger and I can get away."

"Your mother is a former teacher. What's more, she has a heart of gold and the patience of a saint. She probably enjoys being a grandmother."

They had pushed through the heavy pedestrian traffic on Main Street and were walking down Sandpit Road. Sharon said, "Did you hear that they found the backpacker? It'll be in today's paper. Roger's been on the story since Wednesday, and he happens to know they've sent the body to the state pathologist, although they're not releasing the information. There's something unusual about the death." She lowered her voice. "Mother and Roger and I think it has something to do with the Visitors from outer space."

"Is that so?" he murmured.

"Don't mention it to Arch. You know how

he is. Couldn't you gently talk some sense into his head, Qwill?"

"I doubt whether I'm the one to try," Qwilleran said with tact. "How do you explain all this to your youngsters?"

"We tell them the universe has room for many worlds, some with intelligent life. Alien beings are curious about our planet, just as we're interested in getting to Mars and beyond."

"Have your kids sighted any of these . . . Visitors?"

"No, we're away from the water and don't stay up late. Mother says two A.M. is the best time for sightings."

They had reached the Great Dune Motel, and he handed over the tote bag. "Have you been to lunch at Owen's Place?"

"Too expensive. I carry my lunch. Also, my boss is miffed because they're staying at the hotel instead of with us."

Owen's Place stood alone on the west side of the highway, although its stained cedar siding matched that of the motel, antique shop, fudge kitchen, and other enterprises on the east side. It had been a coin-operated laundry for several seasons before becoming an unsuccessful Chinese restaurant. Now, in the large front windows, the red velvet draperies of its bok choy period had been replaced with white louvered shutters. With the parking lot paved, and the Great Dune as a noble background, it looked quite elegant, and Qwilleran looked forward to dining there before the theater.

The chamber of commerce must have offered Bowen a good deal, Qwilleran thought. Otherwise, why would a man with contempt for country folk choose to spend the summer 400 miles north of everywhere? Evidently the lake was the attraction, since he had a boat. A recreation vehicle with a boat hitch could be seen around the rear of the restaurant, as well as a white convertible, both with Florida tags.

Walking back toward Main Street, Qwilleran passed Arnold's Antique Shop—and stopped short. There in the window was the kind of spindly, high-backed antique chair that had been on the float with the sheep. It was a chair design with character, and it aroused his curiosity. He went into the shop. There were several customers, either buying or browsing. According to their dress and mannerisms, Qwilleran could classify them as campers, or wives of sport fishermen, or boaters from the Grand Island Club who had just lunched at Owen's Place.

The lunch crowd was raving about the chef, the quiche, the skewered potatoes, and the "perfectly darling" maitre d'. Arnold himself was everywhere at once. He was an ageless man with tireless energy, but he had a weathered face that looked like the old woodcarvings he sold. Peering over rimless glasses, he sorted the idle browsers from the potential customers and kept an eye on the former.

A long-haired white-and-black dog wagged a plumed tail at the latter. "Good dog! Good dog!" Qwilleran said to him.

"Hi, Mr. Q! Do you like our pooch?" Arnold asked. "He just wandered in one day. A friendly soul! Brings in more business than an ad in your newspaper!"

"What's his name?"

"Well, you see, we bought a job lot of china that included a dog dish with the name Phreddie on it, so we named the dog to match the dish . . . Excuse me."

Arnold went off to take a customer's money. A man was buying a rusty iron wheel, four feet in diameter but delicate in its proportions, with sixteen slender spokes.

"Beautiful rust job, smooth as honey," the dealer told the purchaser. "It threshed a lot of wheat in its day."

Meanwhile, Qwilleran poked through baskets of arrowheads, Civil War bullets, and old English coins. "What's that guy going to do with the wheel?" he later asked Arnold.

"Hang it over the fireplace in his lodge on Grand Island."

"Hmmm ... I could use one of those myself." He was thinking of the gable end above his own fireplace, a large blank wall that had originally displayed a mounted moosehead; its dour expression had been a depressing reminder of animal rights. Later, the wall showcased a collection of lumberjack tools: axes, a peavey, and crosscut saws with murderous two-inch teeth—equally discomforting. A wheel, on the other hand ...

"There were two of them, from a field

combine," Arnold said. "The other one's in my main store in Lockmaster. I'll have it sent up here, but it'll take a couple, three days."

"No rush . . . I'd also like to inquire about the chair in the window. What is it? There were eight of them on a float in yesterday's parade."

"That's a pressed-back dining chair, circa 1900, sometimes thought of as a kitchen chair. In the country, a lot of dining was done in the kitchen. In 1904, or there-abouts, the Sears catalogue offered this chair for ninety-four cents. Did you hear me right? *Ninety-four cents*! They must've sold millions of 'em . . . Pretty thing, ain't it?"

"There's something debonair about it," Qwilleran said.

It was golden oak, heavily varnished, with a hand-caned seat and nine turned spindles—almost pencil-thin—and a deep top rail that had a decorative design pressed into it. Two turned finials on top, like ears, gave it a playful fillip but would be practical handgrips.

The dealer said, "This may have been a knock-off of an earlier and more expensive design—with the top rail carved, and a price tag more like two fifty. The ones I've seen around here are all in the ninety-four-cent class. The seat on this one has been recaned. I'll make you a good price if you're interested."

"I'll think about it," Qwilleran said, meaning that he had no intention of buying. "But I'll definitely come back for the wheel in a couple of days . . . What do you know about the restaurant across the way?" he added as Arnold accompanied him to the door.

"I hear the food's good."

"Have you had contact with Owen Bowen?"

"Only through Derek. He's working there part time, you know. Derek said the entry—where customers wait to be seated—needed some spark. So we put our heads together, and I lent them a setup for the summer months—some Waterford crystal in a lighted china cabinet. We brought it up from the Lockmaster store. And that so-and-so from Florida never picked up the phone to say thank-you, let alone send over a piece of pie. Phreddie has better manners than Owen Bowen!"

* * *

Qwilleran's watch told him that the lunch hour had ended at Owen's Place, and his intuition had told him that Derek would be heading for Elizabeth's Magic to relax and report on events. Qwilleran headed in the same direction, stopping only for a hot dog and two copies of the *Moose County Something.* On the way he thought about another reader-participation stunt: He could take a census of pressed-back chairs in Moose County! . . . Run a photograph of the one at Arnold's . . . Ask, "Do you own one or more of these historic artifacts? Send us a postcard." Arch Riker chaffed Qwilleran about his postcard parties, although he knew very well that subscribers looked forward to the monthly assignments and talked about them all over the county.

On Oak Street there were three contiguous storefronts, each with a windowbox of petunias: Elizabeth's Magic in the center, flanked by a realty agent and a hair stylist. When Qwilleran opened the door, an overhead bell jangled, and three persons turned in his direction: Elizabeth and two customers of retirement age, one tall and one short. They had been his neighbors in Indian Village.

"Ladies! What brings you to the haunts of coot and hern?" he asked.

They greeted him happily. "That's Tennyson!" said the tall one.

"My favorite poem: *The Brook*," said the other.

They were the Cavendish sisters, retired from distinguished teaching careers Down Below. Qwilleran had rescued one of their cats when it became entangled in the laundry equipment. "I hear you're living in Ittibittiwassee Estates," he said.

"Yes, they gave us an apartment with pet privileges."

"We'd never go anywhere without Pinky and Quinky."

"We're here to see the play tonight."

"They have an activities bus that takes residents on day-trips."

"How is Koko?"

"And how is that dear Yum Yum?"

"They find the beach stimulating," he said, "and the screened porch is their university. Koko studies the constellations at night and does graduate work in crow behavior during the day."

"He's such an intellectual cat!" said the tall sister.

"Yum Yum is majoring in entomology but yesterday distinguished herself by saving a life."

"Really?" the sisters said in unison.

"You know how birds knock themselves groggy by trying to fly through a window screen or pane of glass . . . Well, a hummingbird flew into the porch screen and got its long beak caught in the mesh. It was fluttering desperately until Yum Yum jumped to a nearby chairback and gave the beak a gentle push with her paw."

"She's so sweet!" the short sister said.

"Wouldn't you know she'd be a humanitarian?" the other one said.

More likely, she thought it was a bug on the screen, Qwilleran mused.

The bell over the door jangled, and they all turned to see Derek Cuttlebrink barging into the shop. "Just got off work," he announced. "Five hours till curtain time. Got any coffee?" He loped to the rear of the store. Qwilleran followed after exchanging pleasantries with the sisters and giving Elizabeth one of his newspapers.

The two men sat in the black nylon sling chairs with plastic cups of coffee. "I never touch the stuff when I'm on duty," Derek said.

"How's business?"

"Great at lunchtime. I'm not there at night, so I don't know what kind of crowd they get for dinner."

"Do you and your boss hit it off well?"

"Oh, sure. We get along. He needs me, and he knows it. I don't have to take any of his guff." He lowered his voice. "I know more about the food business than he does. At least I've cracked a book or two. He's just a joe who likes to eat and thinks it would be a kick to own a restaurant. They're wrong! It's one of the hardest, most complicated businesses you could pick. Owen happened to latch on to a great chef. She's a creative artist, trained at one of the best chef schools. She's really dedicated! Besides that, she's a nice person—much younger than he is. And not as stuffy. He expects to be called Mr. Bowen. She says, 'Call me Ernie.' Her name is Ernestine. She works like a dog in the kitchen while he goofs off and goes fishing."

"Whatever he happens to reel in, I suppose, goes on the menu as catch-of-the-day. At market price."

"Well . . . no. It's a funny thing, but Owen says Ernie isn't comfortable with lake fish, being a Floridian, so he fishes for the sport. Whatever he catches, he throws back. The guy's nuts!"

"Hmmm," Qwilleran said, smoothing his moustache. "What's your bestseller at lunchtime?"

"Skewered potatoes, hands down."

"I've heard people talk about them. What are they?"

Derek yelled, "Liz, got any skewers left?"

"A few," she said. "I've placed another order, and Mike's turning them out as fast as he can, but we can hardly keep up with the demand."

She showed Qwilleran a set of the foot-long needles of twisted iron with sharp points. At the opposite end each had a decorative medallion for a fingergrip. She said, "If you bake potatoes on skewers, the baking time is shortened, and they're flakier, more flavorful, and more nutritious."

"Who says so?" Qwilleran said. "It sounds like a scam to me."

"I don't know how it originated, but it seems to be an accepted fact. It was Derek's idea to put skewered potatoes on the menu, and Ernie bought a dozen to start. Now she wants more."

"Here's why they're popular," Derek said. "The potatoes are unskewered and dressed at tableside for dramatic effect. Dining in a fine restaurant is part showbiz, you know. People like the special attention they get with tableside service, like fileting a trout or tossing a Caesar salad or flaming a dessert. I do the ritual myself. I put on a good show. Come and have lunch some day."

"I'll do that. Meanwhile, I'm having dinner there tonight before the play."

"That reminds me . . ." He jumped out of his chair and headed for the front door.

"Break a leg!" Qwilleran shouted after him.

"Qwill, have you seen today's paper?" Elizabeth asked. "Look at the announcement on page five."

He unfolded the newspaper he had been carrying and read a boxed announcement:

YOU AIN'T SEEN NOTHIN' YET, HARDLY

Do you like the way folks speak in Moose County?

Do you have pet peeves about English as she is spoken?

Do you think "whom" should be eliminated from the English language?

Are you confused about him-and-me and he-and-I?

ASK MS. GRAMMA

Her column starts next week on this page. Write to her at the *Moose County Something*. Queries and complaints will receive her attention.

"Well, that's a surprise, to say the least," Qwilleran said. "Readers have been clamoring for editorial comment on the sloppy English common in Moose County, but it remains to be seen whether a column on good grammar will accomplish anything. What's your reaction, Elizabeth?"

"Frankly, I think the people who need it most won't read it, and what's more, they see nothing wrong with the way they speak. Their patois was learned from their parents and is spoken, most likely, by their friends."

Qwilleran said, "My question is: Who will write it? Jill Handley on the staff could do it, or some retired teacher of English. But that's Junior Goodwinter's problem. We'll wait and see."

Before going home, Qwilleran drove to Fishport once more. The burlap sack was still covering the sign on the lawn, but there were no police cars in the drive. Qwilleran thought he could knock on the door and ask, as a friend, how things were going. "Is there anything I can do?" was always a key to unlocking confidences.

He knocked on the door, and no one answered. He knocked again. Someone could be seen moving around inside the house—someone who obviously did not want to be bothered. He drove away.

6

Before going to dinner and the theater, Qwilleran fed the cats and treated them to a reading session. They were currently enjoying the sheep book, *Far from the Madding Crowd*. They usually sat on the porch—Qwilleran in a lounge chair, Yum Yum on his lap, and Koko on the back of the chair, looking over his shoulder. If Qwilleran dramatized the story, Koko would get excited and inch forward. Then the cat's whiskers would tickle the man's ear. The episode that Qwilleran read on this occasion was an ear tickler—the tragic event for which the novel was famous.

An inexperienced sheepdog made a fatal mistake. His sire, old George, had the wisdom of a veteran sheepkeeper, but the young one had too much enthusiasm and too little sense. His job was to chase sheep, and he chased them. It was the jangling of bells on fast-running sheep that alerted the farmer one dark night. He called the dogs, and only George responded.

Shouting the shepherd's cry of "Ovey! Ovey! Ovey!" the man ran to the hill. There were no sheep in sight, but the young dog was standing on the edge of the chalk cliff, gazing down below. He had chased the flock until they broke through a hedge and a rail fence and plunged to their death. Lost were two hundred ewes and the two hundred lambs they would have birthed. The farmer was financially ruined, and the poor dog was shot.

Qwilleran slapped the book shut. He had been reading with emotion, and his listeners sensed the tension in his voice. Though it described a nineteenth-century farm in a fictional English county called Wessex, it resembled Moose County, where sheep farming supported so many families. There was a heavy silence on the porch—until the telephone rang.

"Excuse me," he said, dislodging Yum Yum from his lap.

The caller was Sarah Plensdorf, the conscientious office manager at the *Something*. "I'm sorry to bother you on your vacation, Qwill, but I had a request for your phone number from a woman who seemed very young and very shy. When I told her to write you a letter, she insisted that she had an urgent message for you. I took her number and said I'd try to reach you. She was calling from Fishport."

"Give me the number. I'll call her," he said. "You handled it well, Sarah."

"You're to ask for Janelle."

When he phoned the number, a soft, whispery voice said, "Safe Harbor Residence."

He had to think a moment. Was this the home for widows of commercial fishermen? He said, "Is there someone there by the name of Janelle?"

"This is . . . Janelle," she said hesitantly. "Is this . . . Mr. Qwilleran?"

"Yes. You called my office." Her slowness

of speech made him speak in a clipped manner. "You have an urgent message?"

"It's from one of our residents. The widow of . . . Primus Hawley. She's made a lovely . . . gift for you."

He huffed into his moustache. That would be Doris Hawley's mother-in-law. She was embroidering something for him . . . probably *Home Sweet Home* bordered with roses. He glanced at Koko, who was at his elbow, listening. "Very kind of her," he said.

"Would it be too much trouble to . . . pick it up? She's ninety years old. She'd be . . . thrilled to meet you."

Koko was staring at his forehead, and Qwilleran found himself saying, "No trouble at all. I have great respect for the commercial fishing community. I wrote a column on the blessing of the fleet this spring."

"I know! We have it in the parlor . . . in a lovely frame!"

"I'll drop in some day next week."

"Could you come . . . sooner?" she asked in her shy but persistent way.

"Well then, Monday afternoon."

There was a pause. "Sooner?"

"All right!" he said in exasperation. "Some time tomorrow afternoon."

There was another pause. "Could you tell us exactly when? She has to . . . have her nap."

After promising to be there at two o'clock, Qwilleran hung up and was surprised to see Koko running around in circles. "If you could drive," he said to the cat, "I'd send you to pick it up!"

When Qwilleran arrived at Owen's Place, the first thing he noticed in the small foyer was a lighted case of sparkling cut crystal. He looked for a card saying "Courtesy of Arnold's," but there was no credit given. Otherwise the interior was mostly white, with accents of pink and yellow and a great many potted plants, hanging baskets, and indoor trees. He could tell at a glance that they were from The Greenery in Lockmaster, a place that rented plastic foliage for all occasions. Altogether it was not a bad scene: The large casement windows on both long walls were open, and their white louvered shutters framed them pleasantly.

Half the tables were taken, and there

was a hum of excitement from show-goers headed for an opening-night performance. For a beach crowd they were dressed decently, and Qwilleran was glad he had worn his striped seersucker coat. As he stood waiting in the entry, several heads were turned in his direction, and hands waved.

Owen Bowen, handsomely tanned, came forward with a frown wrinkling his fine features. "Reservation?"

"No, sorry."

The host scanned the room. "How many?"

"One."

That required another study of the situation. "Smoking or non-smoking?"

"Non."

After painful cogitation, he conducted Qwilleran to a small table and said, "Something from the bar?"

"Squunk water on the rocks, with lemon zest."

"What was that?"

Qwilleran repeated it and explained that it was a mineral water from a natural spring at Squunk Corners, but he said he would settle for club soda.

The menu was unusual by Moose County standards: veal loin encrusted with eggplant, spinach, and roasted red peppers, with sun-dried tomato demiglaze—that sort of thing. Qwilleran played it safe with a lamb shank osso bucco on a bed of basil fettuccini. The soup of the day was a purée of cauliflower and Gorgonzola served in a soup plate with three spears of chives arranged in a triangle on the creamy surface.

While a self-conscious waitstaff took orders and served the food, the host seated guests and served drinks with an air of zero hospitality. Latticework in the rear of the room screened the bar, the cash register, and a window into the kitchen, where Qwilleran caught glimpses of a young woman in a chef's towering toque. Her face had a look of extreme concentration and a kitchen pallor.

Other diners started leaving at seven-fifteen, saying they were concerned about parking facilities. When Qwilleran arrived at the Botts farm, vehicles lined both shoulders of the highway as far as one could see, and others were being directed into designated pastures. He himself had a press card that admitted him to a lot behind the dairy barn.

Show-goers gathered in the barnyard, reluctant to go indoors. It was a beautiful evening, and this was a festive celebration. The Rikers were there. "How was Owen's Place?" they asked.

Qwilleran was pleased to report that the food was excellent. "The chef is nouvelle, but not too nouvelle. The host is a cold fish. If you don't like cold fish, I suggest you go for lunch, when Derek is on duty." Then, half turning his back to Arch, he asked Mildred, "Has your sensitive husband recovered from the mortification of knitting in public?"

"Don't be fooled, Qwill. He's enjoying the notoriety. He even got a fan letter from a mechanic in Chipmunk."

Arch said, "I hope the play's better than the precurtain conversation. Let's go in."

"Curtain time!" an usher was shouting to the crowd milling about the barnyard.

There was no curtain in the theater, and there were no backs on the seats. Bleachers, providing good sight lines, filled one end of the barn, while an elevated stage occupied the other. Although the set was sketchy, the audience could imagine a fashionable country house with a terrace off to the right.

The lights dimmed; the haunting electronic sounds faded; and the play began—with headstrong characters insisting that UFOs were figments of the imagination. Meanwhile, a spaceship was landing in a rose garden offstage with green lights spilling onstage. Enter: a Visitor from outer space, almost seven feet tall. The audience howled as they recognized their favorite actor. He wore a Civil War uniform and sideburns and explained to the earthlings that he had miscalculated and landed in the wrong century. It was a challenging role for Derek, who was in almost every scene of the play.

During intermission, when the audience was glad to leave the bleachers for a few minutes, Qwilleran listened to their comments:

Elizabeth Hart: "Isn't he talented? He does everything well."

Lyle Compton: "Will that guy ever stop growing?"

Arch Riker: "This play puts UFOs where they belong: in a comic strip."

Junior Goodwinter: "I hear tickets are sold out for three weekends."

Obviously Derek was stealing the show. All his groupies were there, overreacting to every line. After the last act, and after the last tumultuous applause had shivered the timbers of the old barn, it was a joyful crowd that poured out to the barnyard.

Junior grabbed Qwilleran's arm. "How about lunch tomorrow and some shoptalk? I have some ideas to bounce around."

"You come to Mooseville, and I'll buy," Qwilleran said. "I have a two o'clock appointment in Fishport. We'll go to Owen's Place and see Derek in a different role."

Then he found Arch waiting for Mildred. He was standing near an arrow that pointed to the portable facilities behind the barn. Qwilleran said, "Apart from the hard seats, how did you like the show?"

"I hope it's not going to stir up a lot more UFO fever! People have brainwashed themselves, and my wife is one of the nuts."

"Well, I listen to their conversation politely," Qwilleran said, "but I don't buy it, of course."

"I've stopped being polite. Enough is enough! Toulouse sits staring into space, the way cats do, and Mildred insists he's watching for Visitors . . . here she comes now."

"Sorry to keep you both waiting," she said. "There was a long line. Qwill, would you like to stop at our place for a snack?"

"Thanks, but I want to go home and grapple with my review while the show's fresh in my mind."

"We're parked half a mile away," Arch said. "Where are you parked?"

"Behind the barn. Reviewer's privilege."

"Lucky dog! I run the paper, and I have to walk half a mile!"

"I'll make a deal," Qwilleran said. "You write the review, and I'll drive you to your car."

It was no deal.

What Qwilleran missed most about newspaper life Down Below was the interminable shoptalk—in the office, at the watercooler, in the lunchroom, at the Press

Club. So he looked forward to his Saturday luncheon with the managing editor. Junior, for his part, probably welcomed an exchange of ideas with a journalist who was also a friend—and the financial backer of the newspaper in a roundabout way.

Qwilleran arrived in the parking lot of Owen's Place just as Junior was stepping out of his car. They went in together.

"Wow! Some class!" Junior exclaimed as Derek greeted them.

"Good show last night," Qwilleran said. "You hit exactly the right blend of absurdity and convincing reality."

When they were seated, Junior said to Qwilleran, "Do you think the play will kick off any UFO hysteria in Mooseville? You know how they are around here. We don't want to attract any attention from the TV networks or major dailies Down Below. They're quick to pounce on bizarre stories about simple country folk like us. But that's not why Arch has vetoed stories about mysterious lights in the sky. It's a personal phobia."

"What about you, Junior?"

"I have no strong beliefs, one way or the

other, but I maintain that the reaction of beach residents is news, and we should report it—plus a sidebar quoting the Pentagon and other official sources, as the other side of the story."

The drinks were served—one red spritzer and one Squunk water—and Qwilleran raised his glass in a toast. "To sanity, if there's any left!"

"What's your next column, Qwill?"

"A thousand words on the diary of Lisa Compton's great-grandmother. Mark Twain came through here on a lecture tour in the late nineteenth century, and she had a crush on him. They never met, but she fell for his moustache."

"Sounds like hot stuff for a family newspaper," Junior said drily.

"There was one interesting fact: Strange objects in the sky were being reported prior to the 1900s, thought to be from the spirit world . . . Have you looked at the menu, Junior? We'd better order."

Besides imaginative variations on standard luncheon dishes, there was the house specialty: "Try our skewered potato! A flawless 20-ounce Idaho, baked on a skewer and dressed at tableside with three toppings. Choose one sauce, one accompaniment, and one garnish."

The newsmen studied the list of toppings conscientiously:

THE SAUCES: Choice of marinara, Bolognese, Alfredo, ratatouille, curried chicken, or herbed yogurt with anchovies.

THE ACCOMPANIMENTS: Choice of sautéed Portobello mushrooms, red onion rings, pitted ripe olives, garlic-pickled garbanzos, sautéed chicken livers, or grilled tofu cubes.

THE GARNISHES: Choice of grated Parmesan cheese, toasted cashews, shredded carrots with capers, slivered fresh coconut, crumbled Stilton cheese, or sour cream with chives.

After studying the list, Junior said, "It's daunting, to say the least. I can't believe this is happening in Moose County."

"Blame Derek," Qwilleran said. "That's what happens when you send a boy to college."

"What I really wanted was a roast beef sandwich."

Qwilleran called Derek to the table. "Would we be thrown out if we ordered roast beef sandwiches with horseradish?"

"Sure, that's okay," Derek said, adding in a lower voice, "We're short of skewers, anyway."

They spent the lunch hour discussing editorial policies, staff problems, new ideas, and old mistakes. Qwilleran enjoyed it and offered advice, but finally he looked at his watch and said it was time to leave for Fishport.

"What are you doing there?"

"Paying a call on some elderly residents at Safe Harbor. It's one of the many things I do for the *Moose County Something* and don't get paid for. I make an appearance, shake hands, say the right things, and make friends for the paper. I hope it's appreciated."

"I think you like old ladies."

"Why not? They like me," Qwilleran said flippantly, although he realized he was drawn to octogenarians and nonagenarians of both sexes, and he knew why. He had never known his grandparents. His mother never talked about them, and as a kid he was too self-absorbed to ask questions. His life was all about playing baseball, acting in school plays, training for spelling bees (which he always won), and practicing the piano (reluctantly).

There were no birthday cards or Christmas presents from grandparents. His extended family consisted of his mother's friends and Arch Riker's parents. Pop Riker was as good a father as he had ever known. Now he often wondered about his forebears. Who were they? Where did they live? What did they do? Why had his mother never mentioned them? Could they be traced? There was a genealogical society in Pickax; they would know how to proceed.

He thought about it on the way to his afternoon appointment. Before he knew it, he had reached the Fishport village limits, and the landmark mansion called Safe Harbor loomed ahead.

7

Safe Harbor was a three-story frame structure in the Victorian style, with porches, bay windows, balconies, gables, a turret, and a widow's walk. It had been the residence of a shipping magnate in Moose County's heyday, when families were large, travel was slow, and guests stayed a long time. There were many bedrooms upstairs and servants' quarters in the garret. The widow's walk was a small observation platform on the roof with a fancy wrought-iron railing. From that elevation, members of the family could watch for sailing ships bringing loved ones or valuable cargo, all the while worrying about treacherous rocks and lake pirates.

Following the economic collapse, the stately mansion became a boarding house for sandpit workers, then a summer hotel in the prosperous rum-running days, then a private school for sailing buffs from Chicago. Eventually it was purchased by the Scotten, Hawley, and Zander families as a retirement home for widows of commercial fishermen, whose occupation was on the most-dangerous list in government studies.

When Qwilleran arrived and rang the jangling bell on the front door, it was immediately opened by a breathless young woman with a sweet smile. A mass of auburn hair cloaked her thin shoulders. "I'm Janelle Van Roop," she said softly. "It's so . . . wonderful of you to come, Mr. Qwilleran. All the ladies . . . are waiting in the parlor."

It was a large dark foyer with an elaborately carved staircase and double doors opening into equally dark rooms. Janelle led him to the one room that was light and bright and cheerful, with white lace curtains on the tall narrow windows. As they entered, applause came from twelve pairs of frail hands. Twenty-four widows with gray or silver hair and pretty blouses sat in a circle.

Janelle said, "Ladies, this is our . . . beloved Mr. Q!" There was another patter of applause with more enthusiasm than volume.

"Good afternoon, ladies," Qwilleran said in a mellifluous voice that mesmerized his listeners when he pulled out all the stops. "It's a great pleasure to meet so many loyal readers, looking so festive and so . . . fetching."

There were titters of amusement and delight.

"I'd like to shake your hands individually, if Janelle will make the introductions."

There was a general murmur of excitement.

Qwilleran had done this before, and he performed in a courtly manner that appealed to women of a certain age. It was part newspaper public relations and part genuine feeling for the older generation.

As he and Janelle moved clockwise around the room, he cupped each extended hand in both of his—hands that were thin, wrinkled, or arthritic. He held them while he said the right things. He paid compliments, asked questions, and proffered greetings from Koko and Yum Yum. The exploits of the Siamese were often reported in the "Qwill Pen" column, and many of the women inquired about their health. For his part, he murmured a variety of "right things":

"You're looking exceptionally well . . . Is that an heirloom cameo you're wearing? . . . Pink is very becoming to you . . . You have happy eyes . . . Your grandson is quite an artist in metal . . . You have the loveliest white hair I've ever seen."

A few women had canes by their sides; the last in the circle was in a wheelchair. She was introduced as Rebecca Hawley.

"I've made something for you, Mr. Q," she said in a faltering voice. "I've been working on it since last October." She handed him a roll of linen tied with a red ribbon like a diploma.

Concealing his apprehension, he unrolled it slowly, then stared at it in disbelief. The painstakingly embroidered words stared back at him—his own words, stitched in black letters:

CATS ARE CATS . . . THE WORLD OVER!
THESE INTELLIGENT, PEACE-LOVING
FOUR-FOOTED FRIENDS—WHO ARE
WITHOUT PREJUDICE, WITHOUT HATE,
WITHOUT GREED—
MAY SOMEDAY TEACH US SOMETHING.
　　　　　　—THE QWILL PEN

"I'm overwhelmed!" he said. "I don't know what to say!" The words were from his semiannual cat column published the previous fall. "How can I thank you, Mrs. Hawley?"

"Do you like it?" she asked, eager for approval.

"Do I like it! If it had been chiseled in marble, it couldn't have been more of an honor. I'll put it in an important frame and think of you every time I see it."

"Oh, my!" She put her bony hands to her face and rocked back and forth in pleased embarrassment.

Janelle spoke up. "Thank you, Mr. Q, for . . . paying us this visit. We know . . . how busy you are."

"My pleasure!" he said, throwing a final salute to his enraptured fans.

In the foyer Janelle seemed nervous. "Please, Mr. Q . . . somebody wants to see you . . . privately. She's waiting . . . in the office."

"Who is it?"

"You'll see."

The office was a small space under the stairs, equipped with desk, filing cabinet, and two institutional chairs. Perched primly on one of the hard seats was Doris Hawley. She jumped to her feet.

"Mrs. Hawley! What a surprise!" he said.

"I'm sorry—"

"No need to feel sorry. I've been wondering about you . . . Let's sit down. I'm still weak in the knees after seeing your mother-in-law's gift." He waved the roll of linen.

"This was the only way I could think of—to talk to you without being seen . . . Do you mind if I close the door?"

"I'll close it . . . But why the secrecy, Mrs. Hawley?"

Her face made it clear that it was far from a happy secret. "They don't want us to talk to anybody—Magnus and me—and if we talk to the media, we could be arrested. It's a terrible feeling. What have we done? They don't tell us anything."

"You identified the hiker's body?"

"Yes, and they thanked us and apologized, sort of. But the next day the state troopers came to the house with orders from the State Bureau of Investigation: no talking to anybody about anything!"

"Ridiculous!" he said with indignation, although he stroked his moustache questioningly.

"Magnus asked them why we couldn't talk, but all they'd say was 'SBI orders.' The sheriff isn't so bad. We know all the deputies, and the one who comes here goes to our church. She said it was unfair, but they had to follow SBI orders."

"It seems like high-handed treatment," Qwilleran said. "I suggest you remove the burlap sack from your sign and get back into the baking business. And if there's a single objection from the police, have Janelle phone me, and I'll meet you here."

Mrs. Hawley was grateful to the point of tears.

"How does Magnus react?"

"Oh, he's mad! He's furious!"

In the foyer, he said to Janelle, "I'm giving you my private phone number; you may need to call me again . . . Are you a Canary?"

She wore the yellow smock that identified care-giving volunteers in Moose County. "Yes, I'm an MCCC student in health care," she said in her languid way, "and . . . I get credits for . . . community service."

"Good! Your time is well spent here."

He walked to his van, hoping he had said the right thing to Mrs. Hawley and wishing Arch Riker could have seen his performance for the elderly women. Driving home, he pondered the small intrigues that occur in small towns. The SBI had overreacted, assuming that gullible townfolk would panic if faced with something hard to explain—and also assuming, rightly, that the media would jump on the story and blow it up out of proportion.

More mystifying to Qwilleran was Koko's behavior in this, and other situations. The cat had *wanted him* to accept Janelle's invitation; he had sensed some undisclosed reason behind it. In the same way he had *wanted Qwilleran* to take the recumbent bike to the cabin, where it would make a rousing finale to the parade. The latter was a minor matter, but it signified that Koko was tuned in, somehow, to forthcoming events. Uncanny! Likewise, he knew there was something buried in the sand ridge—something that should not be there. All cats have a sixth sense, Qwilleran knew, but in Kao K'o Kung it was developed to an incredible degree!

On the way back to town, Qwilleran's watch told him that Derek might be at Elizabeth's Magic, cooling off after his steamy lunch hour at Owen's Place. Derek had a play to do that evening; there would be theater talk as well as restaurant talk.

Derek had not yet arrived. Elizabeth said he was rearranging the tables, putting some on the diagonal to dispel the effect of a railway dining car. It would be a surprise for the boss.

"Does Owen accept all Derek's ideas?" Qwilleran asked.

"So far he's had carte blanche. Derek charms everyone," she said, her eyes glowing.

Qwilleran had known Derek since his days as a busboy, and always he treated CEOs and visiting bishops with the same offhand bonhomie that captivated the young girls who adored him.

"Have you met Ernie?" Qwilleran asked Elizabeth. "What's she like?"

"Very nice, but she's a person with an intense drive. She was here to buy skewers and she asked about the rune stones, so I did a reading for her."

"What are they exactly?"

"Little stones inscribed with a prehistoric alphabet that's used for divining the future. My reading for Ernie was so negative that I didn't give her an honest interpretation . . . Here comes Derek!"

He blustered into the shop with his usual energy. "I'm thirsty! Got anything cold?" He bounded to the rear, where there was a small refrigerator beneath the coffeemaker, then flopped into a chair with a bottle of chilled grapejuice.

Qwilleran joined him. "Do you have any problem shifting gears from cuisine to showbiz?"

"Nah. It's all showbiz."

"Too bad Ernie can't take an evening off to see you act."

"She'd never go to the theater. She's a workaholic," Derek said. "Works nine-to-nine with only a two-hour break in the afternoon, and then she spends it studying

recipes. Did you see that big recreation vehicle behind the restaurant? It's full of
cookbooks! I tell you, she's a real pro!
Turns out orders fast. Makes presentations
that are works of art. I asked her what she
liked most about her job, and she said 'the
fast pace.' I asked her what she liked least,
and she said 'tomatoes in winter.' That's
the way she is!" Derek glanced at the customers in the shop and said, "Come in the
stockroom."

Among the shelves and cartons and
racks he could speak freely. He knew
Qwilleran liked to hear the story behind
the story. "The way it works, I report at ten-
thirty A.M. Owen is there to check me in.
We count the cash together, and I sign for
it. Then he takes off with his bait bucket for
a few hours of fishing—or that's what he
says. But there's liquor on his breath already! Makes you wonder what he eats for
breakfast. Makes you wonder what's in the
bait bucket. Does he anchor the boat in
some secluded cove where he can nip
schnapps and read porno magazines? Is
that why he never brings in any fish?"

Qwilleran said, "You're getting to be very

cynical for your age, Derek. Does Ernie ever go out in the lake with him?"

"Only on Mondays, when we're closed. And then I'll bet she takes cookbooks to read. Off the record, Qwill, I think she worries about his drinking. She made two stupid mistakes last week because she wasn't concentrating—like making a BLT without the T. Then a Monte Cristo with mushroom sauce didn't have the sauce . . . Well, I've gotta go home and make an adjustment from dumb earthling to smart alien."

He galloped out of the shop, tossing a "see ya later" in Elizabeth's direction.

Driving home along the shore, Qwilleran was beginning to watch for the old schoolhouse chimney and the K sign when he saw a vehicle approach from the east and turn into his drive. He stepped on the gas. It was a green van he could not recognize, and he was wary of uninvited visitors. Yum Yum had been kidnapped once, and he had never forgotten the horror of coming home and finding her gone.

By the time the green van pulled into

the clearing, the brown van was right on its tail, and Qwilleran jumped out to confront the driver.

"Bushy!" he shouted. "Why didn't you let me know—"

Stepping out of the green van was a young man in a green baseball cap: John Bushland, commercial photographer, who also handled assignments for the *Moose County Something*. Losing his hair at an early age—but not his sense of humor—he encouraged friends to call him Bushy.

"I phoned—no answer—so I took a chance. I had a shoot in the neighborhood—a family reunion."

"For the paper?" There were dozens of family reunions every summer weekend, and they rated two inches of space and no photo.

"No, the Ogilvies have a professional group picture taken every year for their family history. For the usual shot of the eldest and the youngest, I posed a hundred-year-old woman and a two-day-old lamb. Cute. What? They thought it was brilliant."

"You've got a new van, Bushy."

"No, a new paint job. Dwight Somers

recommended a less somber color and a livelier logo to enhance my image in a rural environment."

"Business must be good if you can afford a PR man."

"Not that good! I bartered photos for his services."

"Well, come in and have a gin and tonic. I just happen to have the main ingredients."

Bushy leaned on the bar while Qwilleran mixed his drink and opened a ginger ale for himself. "Where are the cats?" he asked.

"Asleep somewhere."

"Then I can speak freely. Those guys are finally licked. I've sent for the trick lens."

For several years Bushy had been trying to take a photo that would win him a prize and land Koko and Yum Yum on the cover of a cat calendar. Having no desire to be cover cats, they had thwarted his repeated efforts with exasperating ingenuity, no matter how stealthy his strategy. Now he had tracked down a vintage lens for photographing reluctant subjects without their knowledge.

"Good!" Qwilleran said. "Those scoundrels have been calling the plays long enough!"

As they carried their drinks to the porch, Yum Yum uncurled from sleep on a chair seat, rising gracefully like a genie coming out of a bottle. Koko had been sleeping compactly in sixty-four-square inches of sunlight on top of his pedestal; he jumped down with a grunt.

The two men stretched out on lounge chairs and absorbed the view: blue sky, white clouds, blue lake with white sails skimming across the horizon.

"That's the Grand Island Club's annual wooden sloop regatta," Bushy said. "Last year's winner wanted me to sail with them this year and shoot, but I wouldn't go out on one of those babies for any amount of money! I'll stick to stink-boats . . . Did you know I've got a new one? Twenty-four-foot cuddy cruiser with depth-finder, VHF radio, stereo. Sleeps four. I'd like to take you for a cruise. I think you'd be impressed."

"You'll never get me out on a boat again, Bushy," Qwilleran said with fervor. "After that trip to Three Tree Island, I had nightmares for a month, and Roger almost succumbed to pneumonia."

"Yeah, well, I've learned a lot since then. I pay attention to the weather clues—the whistling overhead and the sudden change in the sky color. It wouldn't happen again, and we'd pick a nice day."

"We picked a nice day the last time."

That ill-fated voyage had been a fool's errand in the first place, Qwilleran reflected. A pilot flying over the island had seen what he thought were charred circles on the shore. He mentioned the phenomenon to Roger MacGillivray, who was a spaceship buff. Bushy, being another, wanted to cruise out to see them. Qwilleran went along for the ride. They never saw the circles, and it was a miracle that they ever saw the mainland again.

Qwilleran knew the young man was inordinately fond of his new craft. He said, "Okay, I'll put my life on the line, but give me advance notice so I can take out some more insurance."

Bushy said, "I was thinking about tomorrow. The weather's going to be perfect, and I thought we could pick up some pasties at the Nasty Pasty and have lunch on board."

Qwilleran was inordinately fond of pasties. "What time? Where?" he asked.

After Bushy had driven away, Qwilleran brushed the Siamese. They liked it, and he found it conducive to thinking. Yum Yum considered it an exciting game of fight-the-brush; Koko submitted with the dignity of a monarch being robed for a coronation. The porch was ideal for the ritual. Gentle breezes wafted the loose cat hair into corners where it could easily be scooped up. Whimsically he wondered if the balls of soft weightless fluff could be spun into yarn for Arch to knit into socks. What a Christmas gift that would make! Good for a laugh, at any rate.

One thought led to another, and he phoned Mitch Ogilvie, a goat farmer. "I hear you had a family reunion today, Mitch."

The farmer was in the cheesehouse, and his voice had the hollow ring of concrete walls and stainless-steel vats. "I was there long enough to get in the official photo, that's all. Goats don't give you any days off."

"Would you happen to know the two Ogilvie women who do handspinning?"

"Sure, that would be Alice and her daughter. Her husband has the sheep ranch on Sandpit Road."

"If I wrote a column on handspinning," Qwilleran asked, "would she make a good interview? Is she an authority?"

"Definitely. We're going to get some cashmere and angora goats just for her. She sells her yarn to weavers and knitters all over the country. Her daughter has started a unisex knitting club, Qwill. You ought to join."

Qwilleran huffed into his moustache. "Arch Riker has joined, and when he finishes the toe of his first sock, I may consider it. Frankly, I think I'm perfectly safe."

When Qwilleran phoned the sheep ranch, there was no answer; no doubt the family was still at the reunion, enjoying barbecued chicken, baked beans, and potato salad. He chose not to leave a message but applied himself to his theater review for Monday's paper. He sprawled in a lounge chair on the porch, writing on a legal pad while the Siamese napped, the clouds scudded, and the regatta dotted the horizon with white sails.

Writing a review of a small-town play for a small-town theater was a special art. He asked himself, What is the purpose of the review? Not to show off the intellect and educated taste of the reviewer. Not to flatter the amateur actors into quitting their jobs and moving to New York. Not to give away the surprise of the plot and spoil it for next week's audience. And not to convince readers that they were smart to stay home and watch television.

Instead, he told the stay-at-homes what it was like to attend an opening night: the crowd; the excitement; the transformed barn; the stage set; the audience reaction; the pomposity of the major general; the snobbery of the TV commentator; and the roar of laughter when the unexpected happened.

Every once in a while Qwilleran looked up from his pad, and his eyes fell on Koko, after which he went on writing with a fresh idea or neat turn of phrase. It was exactly what Christopher Smart had written about Jeoffrey: *For he's good to think on if a man would express himself neatly*.

In one of these interludes, he saw Koko raise his head suddenly, crane his neck, and point his ears toward the lake, as if a crow had stamped its feet on the beach or a grasshopper had rustled the tall grasses. All was quiet, yet Qwilleran found himself touching his moustache in expectation. A few minutes later a figure rounded a curve in the shoreline and came into view: a young woman in black tights, a leopard shirt, black baseball cap, and jogging shoes. She was not the usual beach-comber in shorts, T-shirt, and sandals. She was not strolling and searching the beach for agates or walking briskly with pumping elbows. She trudged doggedly.

Qwilleran walked to the top of the sand-ladder, where he stood with hands in his pant pockets. When she came close enough, he called out, "Good afternoon! Beautiful day!"

Startled, she looked up, nodded, and labored on, a polished leather bag on a very long strap dangling from her shoulder. That was another item never seen on the beach.

In half an hour she was back, trudging without looking to right or left.

8

When Qwilleran went to the drugstore Sunday morning to pick up his *New York Times*, who should be doing the same thing but Arch Riker. "Had your breakfast?" Qwilleran asked him.

"Sure have! Pecan waffles, apple-chicken sausages, and blueberry muffins," Arch gloated, a not-too-subtle reminder that he was married to the newspaper's food writer. "But I'll have a cup of coffee with you, if you're getting something to eat."

They crossed the street to the Northern Lights Hotel and took a table in the coffee shop, overlooking the harbor. Mrs. Stacy rushed forward to greet them. As co-owner, her job was to keep guests happy; her husband, Wayne, solved the problems.

"Where are the sailboats?" Qwilleran asked her. "Isn't it supposed to be a two-day regatta?"

Her face saddened. "It was called off. There was a drowning yesterday—late."

"There was nothing about it on the newscast last night."

"It was all over the Chicago TV channels. He was the son of a big shot down there. He was an expert swimmer, too, but . . . could I bring you gentlemen some coffee?"

Qwilleran said to Riker sourly, "It wasn't news here because the victim wasn't 'one of us,' as the locals say."

"I'm sure we'll have it in tomorrow's edition."

"Yes, twenty words in the here-and-there column. If he were local, the item would have a front-page headline."

Riker shrugged. "What can I say? I can't defend our policy, but it's the way things are. Sad but true. It's human nature to react more emotionally to a skateboard accident on Sandpit Road than a derailed train

in New Jersey. Why don't you write a column about it?"

"I may do that."

"Have you written your review of the
play? What did you say?"

Facetiously, Qwilleran replied, "I said
that Jennifer was sweet, Kemple was loud,
and Derek was tall. I said the whole cast
had learned their lines and the bleacher
seats were hard."

Arch ignored the flip retort. "Did you explain the name of the theater? Not many
locals will get the joke."

"No need to explain, boss. The few who
know about the Friars Club in major cities
will appreciate the pun. Those who think
our Fryers Club refers to dead chickens
will get a laugh for a different reason, and
no one's intelligence is insulted." He ordered ham and eggs and country fries
without consulting the menu.

"What have you heard from Polly?"
Riker asked, aiming at a more agreeable
topic.

"Just a shower of postcards. She and
her sister Mona are apparently whooping it
up in Ontario."

"Millie and I didn't know she had a sister."

"Mona lives in Cincinnati, and they haven't seen each other for years. Her name is short for Desdemona. Polly's real name is Hippolyta from *Midsummer Night's Dream*."

"I don't blame her for hushing it up."

"Their father was a Shakespeare scholar, and he named his offspring for characters in the plays. Polly has a sister Ophelia and . . ." Qwilleran's attention wandered.

"What are you staring at?"

"A woman sitting alone at a table in the corner. She's the same one who walked along my beach yesterday, looking aloof. She still looks as if she doesn't belong here and wishes she were somewhere else."

"Maybe she just disembarked from a spaceship," Riker said with flagrant sarcasm.

Qwilleran stood up and tossed his napkin on the chair seat. "I'll be back in a minute." He crossed to the table where a woman in a baseball cap was preparing to leave. "Excuse me," he said respectfully, "but are you Dr. Frobnitz from Branchwater University?"

"No," she said curtly.

"I'm sorry. She's due to arrive today, and I'm supposed to meet her. I was sure you were—"

"Well, I'm not!" she snapped, standing and shouldering her handbag with pointed annoyance.

"Please forgive the intrusion," he called after her as she left the coffee shop. To Mrs. Stacy, who had observed the brief encounter, he explained, "I thought she was someone else. Do you know who she is?"

"She's not registered here, but she's been coming here for meals. She must be staying at the hotel. I tried to make her feel welcome, but she's very standoffish."

"That's a good word for it."

Qwilleran looked smug as he returned to his table and the breakfast plate that had been served.

"What was that performance all about?" Riker asked.

"I just wanted to hear her say a few words. I thought she might be from the SBI, investigating the backpacker case, but she sounds more Main Line than bureaucratic."

"For your information, Qwill, that case is

dead in the water. The closure will be in to-morrow's paper: death attributed to natural causes."

"Hmff," Qwilleran murmured. There was more to the mystery than the cause of death, according to Andrew Brodie. He picked up a fork and attacked the fried eggs with burnt edges, the sliver of ham, the warmed-over potatoes, all swimming in grease on a cold plate.

Riker said, "I've come to the conclusion that you simply *like food*, good or bad. When we were kids, you'd shovel it in as if you were starving, no matter what it was."

"I know good food from bad," Qwilleran said, "but I adjust. I happen to know they have trouble getting cooks on week-ends . . . Have you finished knitting your first pair of socks, Arch?"

"Heck, I haven't even reached the heel-flap of the first one."

"How many men are in the knitting club?"

"Four and a half. I'm not in it with both feet. I shouldn't have let Barb Ogilvie twist my arm, but she's young and blond and has sheep's eyes . . . By the way, Millie is making lamb stew and inviting singles to dinner tomorrow night. Why don't you join us? Lisa Compton will be there, because Lyle has a conference in Duluth. Roger is coming because Sharon and the kids and some other homeschoolers are taking an overnight bus trip to a hands-on museum in Lockmaster."

"What time?"

"Six, for drinks. They're coming right from work. How does it feel to be on vacation?"

"What vacation?" Qwilleran asked grumpily. "Go home and read your newspaper."

A dinner invitation from the Rikers was much appreciated, and Qwilleran felt the urge to take Mildred a gift—something from Elizabeth's Magic, where he could also get a cup of coffee superior to the hotel's undistinguished brew. He pushed through the Sunday morning horde of vacationers to Oak Street and found Elizabeth leaving her shop, even though customers were filing in and out.

"Qwill, did you hear the tragic news?" she cried tearfully. "A crewmember in the regatta fell overboard and drowned! Only nineteen! And about to enter Yale!"

"Did you know him?"

"Slightly, but I know his family very well. His father is CEO of a large corporation in Chicago. What's so awful is that he was a strong swimmer, but they couldn't get him out of the water fast enough. The temperature of the lake is lethal, you know. They circled and got back to him in three minutes, but hypothermia had set in, and he was in shock. By the time they got him out of the water, he was unconscious, and they weren't able to revive him. Everyone's devastated!"

"It's sad news," Qwilleran said. "Sailors know about the risks, but who ever expects it to happen?"

"I thought you'd want to know. Most people around here aren't concerned about Grand Islanders unless they're over here spending money," she said bitterly. "My brother's coming to take me to the island."

"Is there anything I can do?" he asked. For a brief moment he saw it as an excuse to postpone his own boating date.

"Thanks, Qwill, but I've been grooming

Kenneth to wait on customers, and Derek will come at two-thirty . . . I must rush down to the pier now."

Qwilleran gave her a warm nod of sympathy, and she hurried away.

Inside the shop the big blond high schooler, suddenly promoted from stockboy to manager, was enjoying his responsibility. He joshed with customers—especially the young ones—and answered questions about the merchandise as if he knew what he was talking about. He took cash or credit cards, operated the computer, bagged purchases properly but said he didn't do giftwraps. Qwilleran, who had decided on rune stones for Mildred, put him to the test.

"What are these pebbles?" he asked.

"Some old guy picks 'em up on the beach and grinds 'em smooth," he said. "Then some other old guy paints magic letters on 'em. You can use 'em to tell fortunes. There's a little book that tells how."

"Have you had your fortune told?"

"Yeah, Elizabeth said I'm gonna make a lotta money if I work hard and use my brain as well as my muscles."

"I'll take a set," Qwilleran said. Mildred would know about rune stones. She could read palms, handwriting, and tarot cards but never read any of them in Arch's presence.

He put the gift in his van and went down the pier to *The Viewfinder*. It was a sleek white cruiser with V-hull and open cockpit. Bushy, obviously pumped up with pride, was waiting for his reaction.

"Neat craft!" Qwilleran said. "Great deck space! What's the horsepower? How many does it sleep?"

Bushy pointed out the two-person helm station, the well-engineered storage space, and the amenities below deck: four berths, a slick head, and galley with refrigerator, stove, and sink. "I've gotta work a lot harder to pay for this baby," he admitted.

With both men seated behind the windshield, the craft moved slowly out of the dock, putting on exhilarating speed when open water was reached.

"This bucket really moves!" Qwilleran said.

"And steers like a dream," Bushy boasted.

"Good visibility of the water."

"Did you see the compass and depth-finder?"

"What's our destination?" Qwilleran asked as the boat skimmed over the glassy lake in a world of its own.

"Traffic picks up Sunday afternoon," Bushy said, "but I thought this would be a nice time to go out to the lighthouse." He pointed out islands, shoals, and fishing banks and knew their names.

Near the Pirate Shoals, they spotted a cabin cruiser and a speedboat lashed to-gether, starboard to starboard.

"What's that all about?" Qwilleran asked.

"Looks like some kind of hanky-panky. Take the glass, Qwill, and see what you can see."

Training the binoculars on the tête-à-tête, he reported, "No one visible in either boat. Maybe they're below in the galley, making bacon, lettuce, and tomato sandwiches."

"Ha!" Bushy said in derision. "Can you see a name on the transom of the cruiser?"

"It looks like *Suncatcher*. Does that ring a bell?"

"Nah. I don't hang around the marinas. Also, it could be from some other harbor. Any fishing rods in evidence?"

"There's one in a holder, and it's bobbing. They've got a bite, but they don't want to burn the bacon."

"I'll circle around, so you can see the name on the speedboat."

It was an older craft and not as shipshape as the *Suncatcher*. Its name was *Fast Mama*.

"Whoo-ee!" Bushy said.

There was no registration tag visible, an omission that reminded Qwilleran of an uncomfortable day-cruise he had taken when he was a newcomer at the lake. The *Minnie K* was an old tub that docked downshore in the bulrushes because it had not passed inspection and was operating illegally. He said to Bushy, "Let's take off before they get the idea we're tabloid journalists and start shooting at us."

The Viewfinder moved quietly away and a few minutes later passed the south end of Breakfast Island, restored to its wilderness state after a failed attempt at development. Farther up the shore the island changed its name to Grand Island, and there was a marina with yachts and sailboats from Chicago. Beyond that were the palatial "cottages" of summer people from Down Below—the ones who would boat over to Mooseville and spend money at Owen's Place and Elizabeth's Magic. At the north end, the lighthouse stood on a rock-bound promontory, site of so many early shipwrecks. Now there were ringing buoys to warn craft away from submerged dangers.

"Here's where we'll anchor," Bushy said.

Pasties were a perfect easy-to-eat picnic food, and the Nasty Pasty had packed individual cans of tomato juice, apples, coconut cupcakes, and a thermos of coffee.

Qwilleran said, "For a landlubber from Lockmaster, Bushy, you know your way around these waters pretty well."

"You've got me wrong, Qwill. I was born and brought up near the lake. I relocated in Lockmaster when I married. Believe me, it's good to be back here. I have a passion for fishing and boating. You probably never heard this, but my family was in commercial fishing for three generations before my grandfather sold out to the Scottens. He was always telling me about the herring business in the twenties and thirties. They used wooden boats and cotton nets—and no echo sounders or radio phones. You wouldn't believe what fishermen went through in those days."

"Try me," said Qwilleran, always curious about someone else's business.

"Well, the Bushland Fisheries regularly shipped hundred-pound kegs of dried salted herring Down Below, salt being the preservative in those days, before refrigeration. And here's the interesting part: The kegs went to Pennsylvania, West Virginia, and other coal-producing states, and the miners practically lived on herring. They could buy it for four cents a pound. The fishermen got a penny a pound and worked their tails off to get it. They were up before dawn, out on the lake in open boats in all kinds of weather, hauling heavy nets till their backs nearly broke, filling the boats to the gunnels with fish, and racing back to shore to dress it. Sometimes they worked half the night—salting it, packing it, and loading it on a freight car before the locomotive backed up and hauled the car away."

Qwilleran said, "I hope they didn't use gill nets."

"No way! They used coarse-mesh 'pond' nets. That's spelled p-o-u-n-d. I never found out why it was pronounced the way it was. In the spring, after the ice broke up, they drove stakes in the lake bottom—tree trunks as long as fifty feet—and they drove 'em with manpower before the gasoline derrick came into use. After that, they set out their nets and visited them every day to scoop out the catch. When cold weather came, they pulled up the stakes before the ice could crush 'em. Then they spent the winter mending nets and repairing boats."

"I can see why your grandfather wanted to get out of the business," Qwilleran said.

"That wasn't the reason. He wasn't afraid of hard work. It's a sad story. He lost his father and two older brothers in a freak incident on the lake. They went out in a thirty-five-foot boat, the *Jenny Lee*, to lift nets. The weather was fair. Lots of boats were in the fishing grounds, all within sight of each other. Suddenly the *Jenny Lee* vanished. One minute she was seen by other fishermen; the next minute she was gone. The authorities searched for a week and never found the bodies—never even found the boat under water. The whole village of Fishport was in mourning. It's remained an unsolved mystery."

Qwilleran stared at Bushy sternly. "Is this an actual fact?"

"It's the God's truth! There's a memorial plaque in the churchyard. Someone wrote a folksong about it."

"Were there any speculations as to what happened?"

"All kinds, but there was only one conclusion, and you won't like it, Qwill. It had to have something to do with the Visitors—like, they could make a thirty-five-foot boat vaporize. There were lots of talk about the Visitors way back then, you know: Blobs of green light in the night sky . . . Sometimes shining things in daylight. That was before I was born, and they're still coming back—some years more than others."

Qwilleran wanted to believe his friend, but he found it difficult. He said, "You once told me about some kind of incident when you were out fishing."

"Yeah, it was my old boat. I was on the lake all by myself, fishing for bass. All at once I had a strange feeling I wasn't alone. I looked up, and there was a silver disc with portholes! I had my camera case with me, but before I could get out my camera, the thing disappeared in a flash. Their speed, you know, has been clocked at seventeen hundred miles per hour."

Qwilleran listened with his usual skepticism, although he tried not to show it. He thought, Here I am in the middle of the lake with a crazy guy! Watch it!

Soberly, he asked, "Do they accelerate from zero to seventeen hundred in the blink of an eye? Or do you think they have a technology that makes them invisible at will?"

"That's the mystery," Bushy said. "Obviously they're far ahead of us technologically. I also have a current theory. Would you like to hear it?"

"By all means."

"You know how the beach has changed this summer—not just in front of your cabin but for miles along the north shore? The loose sand has blown up into a ridge, all the way from Fishport to Purple Point. Okay . . . Now flash back to the time when the spacecraft was right over my head; when it zoomed away, there was a rush of air more powerful than anything I've experienced in a hurricane! It was a single mechanically produced blast that lasted only a second or two."

"Are you suggesting that one or more spacecraft followed the line of the shore, rolling up sand like a carpet?"

"You've got it! I wrote a letter to the paper about my theory, but it wasn't printed."

Qwilleran threw in a handy platitude that seemed appropriate and noncommittal. "We all tend to deny what we don't understand and don't want to believe."

"Exactly," Bushy said with a look of triumph that was followed by silent indecision. Qwilleran waited for the next revelation. "I don't know whether I should tell you this," the young man finally ventured. "It's confidential, but . . . Roger won't mind if I let you in on it."

Qwilleran agreed. The three of them had surely bonded during the Three Tree Island ordeal.

"Well, Roger has access to the sheriff's office, you know . . . and there was something unusual about the backpacker's body when it was found. It was sent to the state pathologist, but they don't have any answers. Naturally they won't admit it, so they're saying the case is closed . . . Now, here's my point: The body was found *in the rolled-up hill of sand*, so . . . you can put two and two together."

"I see what you mean," Qwilleran said, meaning just that and nothing more. He could have revealed who found the body in the hill of sand. Instead he said, "Bushy, this has been a great outing! Thanks for inviting me. You've got a gem of a boat."

The two men were pensive as *The Viewfinder* skimmed across the miles to shore. At the Pirate Shoals, the *Suncatcher* and *Fast Mama* had concluded their tryst and departed. The Sunday-afternoon skippers were swarming over the lake. Qwilleran was thankful to be back on dry land.

Driving back to the cabin, he looked forward to the serenity and sanity of the domestic scene, and he received a tail-waving, ankle-rubbing welcome. Koko had been on the bookshelves, sniffing titles, and had dislodged a book as a subtle reminder that they were entitled to a Sunday-afternoon reading session. It was a Mark Twain novella, *A Horse's Tale*, about an army horse named Soldier Boy, who saved a young girl from wolves. It was a good choice, lending itself to the sound effects that would excite the Siamese: neighing, whinnying, snorting, stomping, and, of course, the howling of a wolf pack. Qwilleran could do them all well, and they gave realism to the melodramatic narrative.

9

On Monday morning Qwilleran faxed his theater review for that day's edition and the "Qwill Pen" for Tuesday, and he started thinking about the "Qwill Pen" for Friday. For him the treadmill effect was the challenge and fascination of journalism. The job was never finished. There was always another deadline. He remembered the newsdesks in metropolitan papers Down Below, where there was always another scandal, another war, another ballgame, another fire, another murder, another election, another court trial, another hero, another obituary, another Fourth of July.

Now, 400 miles north of everywhere, he was seriously considering such topics as the number of pressed-back chairs in the county and the possibility of spinning cat hair into yarn. His old friends at the Press Clubs around the country would never believe it . . . What matter? He was enjoying his life, and when Polly returned from Canada, he would enjoy it more.

First thing Monday morning, knowing that farmers rise with the sun, Qwilleran called Alice Ogilvie at the sheep ranch. He remembered her as the demure pioneer woman on the float, in a long dress with a wisp of white kerchief at the neckline and a modest white cap on severely drawn-back hair.

The woman who answered the phone had a vigorous voice and outgoing personality. "That'll be fun!" she said. "Why don't you come this morning? Bring some cat hair with you if you want to. From one pound of angora rabbit hair you can spin about forty thousand yards, so . . . who knows?"

Then and there Qwilleran forgot about Arch's Christmas gift; it would take forty years to accumulate even a half-pound of the weightless stuff that Koko and Yum Yum were in the habit of shedding. He accepted her invitation to come for coffee and doughnuts, however, and drove to the ranch directly after faxing his copy. It was on Sandpit Road, two miles south of the shore. Having written about sheepkeeping in the past, he knew what to expect: hilly, rocky land unsuitable for crops . . . fences dividing it into pastures . . . ewes grazing peacefully . . . border collies herding flocks from one pasture to another. It was like a game of musical chairs that gave the sheep a change of diet or a rest period with shade, water, and the necessary salt. Lazy rams occupied one enclosure; hyperactive lambs were in another.

Furthermore, Qwilleran knew that the pastoral scene was being managed by computer in the farmhouse. It not only dictated the movement of the flocks but kept records of the animals by number. Instantly available was information on breeding and lambing history, weaning, growth, quality of fleece, genetic background, and even individual eccentricities such as fence jumping.

"What impresses me most," he had written in his column, "is the magic of wool: how a roly-poly sheep can emerge from the shearing shed as skinny as a rail and then grow it all back in the cold months."

The Ogilvies' sprawling old farmhouse gave no sign of being on-line. When Qwilleran drove up, he was met by Alice, in jeans and a western shirt. She ushered him through the side door into a large kitchen with a ten-foot table and a fleet of tall, stately, shiny pressed-back chairs.

"Handsome chairs!" he said. "It was an inspiration to use them on the float."

"It was my daughter's idea. These belonged to my husband's grandparents, back in the days when farmers had large families and lots of hired hands to feed. I don't know how many times they've been varnished and recaned, and they're still on duty, always standing at attention."

"And where did you find a shepherd who can play the flute like Rampal?"

"Wasn't he good? He's head of music at Mooseland High and loved doing it. Why does everyone like to be in a parade?"

They sat around a corner of the big table for coffee and doughnuts. They were real fried-cakes, prepared that morning because Alice was taking them to a coffee hour at the church. Qwilleran had to control his enthusiasm and downright greed.

He said, "I've been reading *Far from the Madding Crowd* and find myself identifying with sheepkeepers."

"Our family," Alice said, "has worn out three copies of that book, over the years. How did you react to the cliff tragedy?"

"With shock and horror."

"It's surprising how little sheepkeeping has changed in two centuries. We still use sheepdogs. The shepherd still moves into the barn when the ewes are lambing. We still call the flock by shouting 'Ovey! Ovey!' Did you know that cry comes from the Latin word for sheep? It's been handed down through eight thousand generations. You know, ewes have an age-old tranquility that rubs off on their humans. I can't help loving the girls, as we call them, and their gentle, trusting, dopey look!"

"I'm glad I brought my tape recorder," Qwilleran said as he prepared to ease her into the subject of spinning. "What do you spin other than wool?"

"Silk, cotton, angora from rabbits, even a little dog hair blended with other fibers.

It's hard-wearing. For socks, you know . . . Want to see the spinning studio where I give lessons?"

The spinning wheel used on the float caught his eye. It had a ten-spoke fly-wheel, tilted bench with treadle under-neath, and a post holding a cornhusk bobbin. A hundred years old, Alice said. Built of pine, cherry, maple, and poplar.

On a table was a thick blanket of fleece, exactly as it came from a ewe on shearing day—white on the inside, weathered on the outside. Alice said it would be torn apart and laundered before being carded and fluffed up like cotton candy. Finally it would be combed and rolled into rovings to feed into the spinning wheel.

She said, "There are weavers and knit-ters who won't work with anything but handspuns."

She demonstrated at a contemporary wheel—compact, with well-engineered head assembly and proper bobbin. Tread-ling with a stockinged foot, she pinched fibers from a roving to feed with rhythmic movements of both hands, all the while talking of ratio, tension, ply, and texture. She invited Qwilleran to try it.

"No, thanks," he said. "I want to preserve my innocence."

He thought she talked like one who has given numerous talks to clubs. "Women used to spin yarn, weave cloth, make garments for the family, cook meals in the fireplace, scrub clothes in a brook, carry pails of water from a spring, and walk miles to church on Sunday."

Outside the window a pickup truck came to an abrupt stop, a door slammed, and footsteps came down a hall.

"My daughter," Alice explained. "She's been in Pickax, renewing her driver's license." She appeared in the doorway, frowning. "Qwill," her mother said, "this is my daughter, Barbara."

"Call me Barb," the young woman said with a pout. "I hate Barbara."

Her mother smiled and shrugged. "By any name she's my one and only daughter and a very talented knitter. She'll tell you all about it. I have to take my doughnuts to the church."

As soon as she had left, Barb said, "I need a drink! I had to wait two hours at the license bureau. Twenty people waiting, and only one guy on duty! . . . what do you drink?"

"Ginger ale, or a reasonable facsimile."

"Well, I'm gonna have rum and orange juice."

She had long straight blond hair and the sultry eyes that Riker had mentioned. They were heavy with makeup, and she shifted them from side to side as she talked—half smiling when Qwilleran complimented her on the knit vest she was wearing. Worn over a white shirt and shorts, it was white with a multicolor pattern of fireworks in the stitchery.

She smokes, Qwilleran thought, recognizing the slightly husky voice.

"Do you smoke?" she asked. "Let's go out on the porch. Alice doesn't let me smoke indoors."

They carried their drinks to the side porch, where Barb sat cross-legged on a glider.

"Tell me about the knitting club," he asked.

"It's unisex. We get together once a week around our big kitchen table, and we laugh a lot—and learn. Then I have a knitting day-camp for kids every Saturday. We have a picnic lunch, and they get several breaks to run around and blow off steam. Then it's back to the needles."

"What do they knit?"

"Socks. Goofy socks. The goofier, the better. They love 'em! Socks are a good way to begin knitting—you learn as you go, and they don't take much yarn."

"What makes a sock goofy?"

Barb jumped off the glider. "I'll show you. I make 'em to sell at Elizabeth's."

She returned with a boxful of mismatched pairs in wild mixes of colors and patterns: stripes, plaids, zigzags, and confetti dots—some with cuffs or tassels.

"Do people actually buy these?"

"As fast as I can knit them. Vacationers buy them to save for Christmas presents because they're different and because they're knitted of handspun wool from local sheep. Each pair of socks has the name of the ewe that grew the wool."

He looked at her askance.

She shrugged. "What does it matter? Sheep all look alike if you don't know them personally. It's just a gimmick." She swiveled her eyes mischievously. "I also have nongoofy stuff on display at Elizabeth's—vests, scarfs, mittens, hats . . . Ready for another drink?"

As she went to the kitchen, he reflected that he had never seen her knits at Elizabeth's because he always avoided the women's clothing section. When he bought gifts for Polly, Elizabeth selected them.

"Where have you been hiding your talent in the last few years?" he asked when she returned with her second drink.

"I've been living Down Below. I came home a couple of winters ago," she said with a shrug of dissatisfaction.

"Why did you leave in the first place?" He had a feeling there was a story behind the story here, and she was getting relaxed enough to tell it.

She slouched down on the glider. "You really wanna know? . . . My girlfriend and I decided there weren't any interesting guys around here, so we went to Florida. But it's hard to get a job there. They think you'll quit as soon as snow melts up north. My girlfriend cuts hair, so she can always get work. I didn't have much luck, though. But then I met a cool guy who was a balloon-chaser!" Her eyes swiveled pleasurably at the recollection.

"What kind of balloons did he chase? And did he ever catch any?" Qwilleran quipped.

She was not sure how to take it. "Mmmm, you know, hot-air balloons? . . . They lift off and drift away, and the pilot never knows where he's gonna land. The chaser follows in a truck so he can pick up the passengers and the envelope and the basket. Our envelope was red-and-white stripes. Our basket held four people standing up."

"Did you become a chaser yourself?"

"I worked weekends in the support crew. Other days I waited on tables."

Qwilleran said, "It seems to me that the pilot has all the fun, and the chaser does all the work."

"No, no! It's exciting! Never knowing where you are—driving miles and miles, zigzagging all over the map, talking to the pilot on the phone, and sort of afraid you'll end up in a swamp."

"If you found it so thrilling, why did you come home?"

She lowered her eyes. "My girlfriend got married. My balloon-chaser wasn't all that interested in a country girl. Then I started dating an older man who really liked me, only . . . I found out he was married. So I came home . . . Why am I telling you all this? I guess it's because I don't really have anybody to talk to."

"How about your mother?"

"Alice is too busy," she said with a shrug.

"But you should be happy. You're doing creative work. You're using your talent. That should be satisfying," he said sympathetically.

"It isn't enough. I don't have anybody I really like—that's the bummer!"

Another truck turned into the driveway.

"Here's Alice," she said. "Gotta empty the ashtray."

Qwilleran drove back to town thinking that the plight of an ex-balloon-chaser was more interesting than the construction and operation of antique spinning wheels, though less suitable for his column.

In Mooseville, he proceeded to wait for the newspaper truck from Pickax; the Monday edition would carry his theater review, the closure of the backpacker case, and something about the drowned sailor from Grand Island. He was curious to know if his remarks to Arch about twenty-word coverage had made any difference. Probably not, he guessed. The truck from the printing plant was always late on Mondays, a breach he attributed to Monday Morning Flu, which seemed to be epidemic in the workplace everywhere. Fortunately, one could always kill time at the Northern Lights Hotel, open seven days a week and twenty-four hours a day. Its presence was like a beacon shining across a somnolent resort town on Mondays, when most places were closed. One could always buy a magazine in the lobby, chat with the desk clerk, sit on the rear veranda to watch the harbor traffic, or have a meal— not a good one, but adequate. The couple who now owned it did their best. Wayne Stacy was conscientious, and his wife was compassionate; she would rather lose customers than discharge the old cook before his retirement. The ordinariness of the food was a tradition to townfolk; to vacationers it was local color.

Qwilleran, always amazed that the historical building had not burned down or slid into the harbor, mounted the broad flight of wooden steps to the wide porch that overlooked Main Street.

"Coming for lunch?" Mrs. Stacy greeted him in the lobby. She always looked businesslike in a neutral-colored pantsuit, but she had a family-style approach. It convinced Qwilleran that she cared more about his hunger than the selling of a lunch.

"I might have a sandwich," he said. "What's the chopper doing over the lake?" The sheriff's helicopter could be seen in the distance, making wide circles.

"Looks like a boating emergency. I hope it's nothing serious. By the way, you know that woman you spoke to in the coffee shop yesterday? She's been in twice more."

"She must like your food," he said, a remark with ambiguous connotations.

"I don't know about that. She eats like a bird."

Qwilleran had his ham-and-cheese sandwich and a cup of cream of tomato soup, and still the Monday papers had not arrived, so he sat in one of the weathered chairs on the veranda and watched the desultory activity on the waterfront.

The helicopter was still hovering, and after a while he began to have uncomfortable feelings about its mission. He patted his moustache several times, and his suspicions were confirmed when an ambulance drove to the end of the main pier and waited. A cabin cruiser was heading for shore at a fast clip. When it docked, a sheriff's deputy jumped to the wharf and conferred with the medics. A wheelchair was rolled out, and a young woman in deckwear and a visored cap was helped off the boat. Although not noticeably ill or injured, she was wheeled to the hotel's side door on the lower level.

At this point, Qwilleran's curiosity exceeded his interest in Monday's paper. He returned to the lobby in time to see an elevator door open and a medic hurry to the manager's office; the other stayed in the elevator with the woman, who was still wearing dark glasses. Mrs. Stacy was brought to the elevator, and a pantomime ensued: questioning, advising, urging, refusing. As a result, she hurried back to her office and the elevator ascended with the patient and the two attendants.

Now captivated by the melodrama, Qwilleran stationed himself where he could see both elevator and office. Mrs. Stacy was making urgent phone calls, to judge by her nervous gestures. The elevator signal indicated that the car had stopped at the second floor. Soon after, Mrs. Stacy left her office and ran up a nearby flight of stairs, whereupon the elevator came down with the emergency personnel and a folded wheelchair.

Still the bundle of newspapers had not arrived, and the desk clerk explained to Qwilleran with a sly smirk, "The truck drops the first bundle here, the next at the drugstore, and third at the tavern, where the driver has a nip of something. Maybe today he's doing it the other way around."

Qwilleran disliked waiting for his newspaper, but the charade piqued his curiosity. Soon he saw Derek Cuttlebrink rushing into the building and bounding up the stairs, after which Mrs. Stacy came slowly down the same flight, looking disturbed.

Qwilleran called to her, "Mrs. Stacy! What's wrong? Is there anything I can do?"

It was the password that always opened the door to confidences.

"Come in the office, Mr. Q, and have a cup of coffee," she said. "I need one. I feel so sorry for that poor woman." She peered across the lobby. "There's my husband. I'm so glad he got back . . . Wayne! Wayne! Come in here!"

The hotelkeeper joined them, nodding to Qwilleran. "Just got back from Pickax. I could smell bad news, soon's I parked in the lot—people standing around, staring at nothing, looking bewildered. What happened?"

"One of our guests drowned!" his wife said. "Owen Bowen!"

"No! . . . I hope he wasn't fool enough to jump off his boat for a swim. I warned him! But he was so cocksure of himself. Any details?"

"Nothing much. He and Mrs. Bowen were boating on their day off, and she radioed for help. The sheriff's marine patrol brought her and the boat in. The helicopter's been searching for more than an hour."

"Where is she now?"

"Upstairs. She wouldn't have a doctor—

afraid he'd give her a shot. She's fussy about what she takes into her body."

"Does she have any friends in town? They haven't been very sociable."

"I don't know," Mrs. Stacy said. "She asked me to call their assistant manager. I had a terrible time finding him."

Wayne Stacy, who was president of the chamber of commerce, said, "I wonder if there's something the chamber can do for her. The restaurant may never reopen. And after all the work we did! Darn shame!"

Qwilleran spoke for the first time. "The chef is called the kingpin of a restaurant, and this one is dedicated to her profession, so she might decide to carry on. Derek Cuttlebrink has been managing the lunch hour, and he could take over both shifts—after the run of the play, of course; he has a lead role."

"Yes, but will that poor woman have the heart to carry on?" Mrs. Stacy worried.

"You know what they say," he reminded her. "Work is a healthy way of coping with grief, and Derek calls her a workaholic. I predict the operation will continue after a suitable hiatus."

"I hope so. The town needs a place like that. They say she's a wonderful chef."

Next he walked to Elizabeth's Magic on Oak Street. Although it was closed on Mondays, she would be there, rearranging her stock and totaling the previous week's receipts. Her enterprise was doing well. She brought to it an infectious spirit, off-beat ideas, and a certain shrewdness. He rapped on the glass, and she ran to the door.

Her first breathless words were, "Qwill! Have you heard—?"

"Shocking, isn't it? How did you find out?"

"Mrs. Stacy was trying to locate Derek, and he happened to be doing some work for me. He rushed over to the hotel."

"Do you expect him to come back?"

"He'd better come back!" she said firmly. "He can't leave me with all this sawdust and plaster lying around!" A somewhat tilted rectangle had been cut in the sidewall of the shop. "I own the whole building, you know, and my tenant next door has moved out, so I'm going to use the space for a lending library."

"Admirable idea!" he said. "But was that

lopsided doorway intentional? Or was Derek hung over?"

Before she could answer, Derek opened the front door with his own key and charged into the shop saying, "Weird accident! You won't believe it."

The three of them huddled in the chairs at the rear as he told what he knew:

"They went out in the boat and anchored somewhere and had a picnic lunch. Ernie had some red wine and got tipsy, so she went below for a nap, leaving Owen to do some fishing. Suddenly she woke up because the boat was rocking violently. Also, her hands and feet were numb. She was scared."

"Awful feeling," Elizabeth said. "I've had it happen after drinking."

"She called to Owen, and he didn't answer. She crawled up the ladder on her knees and elbows, and he was gone! Then she really panicked, and the blood rushed back to her extremities. She radioed for help . . . That's all I know."

Qwilleran said, "I saw them bring her into the hotel in a wheelchair. How did she seem when you arrived, Derek?"

"In a daze. I had to drag the story out of her."

"Did she have an explanation of his disappearance?"

"Yeah. He'd been drinking a lot. Booze—not just wine. She thinks they got caught in the wake of another boat, and he lost his balance and fell overboard."

"Could be," Qwilleran said, although a nagging sensation in the roots of his moustache was telling him, Not so! Not so!

Derek said, "I imagine she'll want to sell the boat; it was Owen's plaything. What she likes is the RV. It has all her cookbooks, and it's kind of cozy. Sleeps two. Has running water. I think she'd be happy living in the thing."

"Well, I've got commitments to take care of," Qwilleran said. "I'll leave you two to clean up the plaster dust."

10

Halfway between the unhappy news about Owen Bowen and the happy prospect of dinner with the Rikers, Qwilleran received a phone call that left him with mixed reactions.

Wetherby Goode, the WPKX meteorologist—whose real name was Joe Bunker—had been his neighbor in Indian Village, and he was good company. An unstoppable extrovert, he announced his weather predictions in song or verse, played cocktail piano at parties, and boasted about being a native of Horseradish in Lockmaster County, once the horseradish capital of the Midwest. Like Qwilleran, a divorced man, he lived alone—with a male cat named Jet Stream.

Earlier in the year Wetherby had talked about his cousin, Dr. Teresa Bunker, a corvidologist at a Southern university. She wanted to produce an animated feature film about crows and was looking for a collaborator. In a weak moment, Qwilleran said he would be interested. Crows were a prominent feature of the environment in Moose County. They strutted around his backyard in Pickax and on the beach in Mooseville; they cawed in the woods incessantly and had flying battles with hawks and blue jays. Unlike pigeons in the city, they were tolerated, however, and Koko was particularly fond of them.

Wetherby had said that his cousin would be coming up to visit her family in the summer and would like to meet Qwilleran and discuss a scenario for the film. Summer had seemed a long way off at the time, but now it was here, and Wetherby was calling to say, "She's coming! She's coming!"

"Who's coming?" Qwilleran demanded,

wrested from his speculations about Owen's drowning and Ernie's immediate future.

"My cousin Tess! She's driving up. She's already left. I don't know her itinerary, because she has relatives and old schoolmates to visit. Besides, she changes her mind easily. However, I gave her your number at the beach, so you two can plan a meeting that's convenient. She knows your cabin, by the way. She used to visit a friend at Top o' the Dunes, and they'd walk on the beach and gawk at the Klingenschoen cabin. That was when the old lady lived there."

"Tell me something about your cousin," Qwilleran asked, thinking he should have asked the question a few months earlier.

"Well, she's a little younger than I am. A big girl. A lot of fun. Likes to do things on the spur of the moment. She was married once, to another academic, but she's an incorrigible optimist, and he was a card-carrying pessimist, so they drove each other crazy."

Fighting his compunctions, Qwilleran managed to say, "Okay, I'll expect her call."

He thought, I can spare an afternoon, or even a day, for a cousin of Wetherby Goode. Then he added, "It'll be a challenge. I've never met a corvidologist."

"So how's the vacation?" his friend asked. "Are you renting your new guest house to Visitors from outer space?"

"Ninety-five percent of sightings," Qwilleran shot back, "are weather balloons, and the other five percent are low-flying fireflies . . . By the way, what does Dr. Bunker drink?"

"Anything, but she's crazy about mint juleps . . . And call her Tess. She likes to be called Tess."

Qwilleran fed the cats early and announced, "I'm having dinner with Uncle Arch and Aunt Mildred. I'll be home around dark, and we'll sit on the porch and look at the stars."

They regarded him with mystification. Yet his mother had always said, "Jamie, it's common courtesy to tell your family where you're going and when you expect to return." Now, after decades of living without a family, he found himself extending this common courtesy to the Siamese. Of course, they had no idea what he was saying, but he felt better for having said it.

He started down the beach carrying a canvas tote bag with the Pickax Public Library logo and marveling at the ever-changing aspect of the lake. This evening, the sky and water were turquoise, and a low cloud bank on the horizon resembled a mountain range. Flirtatious waves made passes at the primly pebbled beach. At Seagull Point, broad wings wheeled over the water. Farther along, cottagers sat on their decks and waved.

At Sunny Daze, Arch was waiting at the top of the sandladder, and Qwilleran handed him two bottles of wine from the canvas bag.

"What else have you got in that thing?" Arch asked with the permissible nosiness of an old friend.

"None of your business," Qwilleran replied with the same liberty. Then he asked Lisa Compton, who was there without her husband, "How's life without Lyle?"

"Serene!" she answered promptly.

"What are the superintendents doing in Duluth? Inventing new ways to give teachers a hard time?"

"Actually, they're coordinating policies on homeschooling."

"Does he approve of it?"

"He says Abraham Lincoln did it, and Thomas Edison did it, and they turned out okay."

"That sounds like Lyle," Qwilleran said. "To tell the truth, I don't know how home-schooling works."

"Ask me!" said Roger MacGillivray. Mildred's son-in-law was a pale young man with a clipped black beard and plenty of enthusiasm. "We follow a prescribed curriculum. Kids get their lessons by E-mail. They take achievement tests. They learn at their own pace with no time wasted on the school bus."

Lisa said, "I wish I'd been home-schooled. I was the only Campbell in a classful of Macdonalds, and they were still avenging the Glencoe Massacre of 1692."

Qwilleran asked, "But do kids get a chance to mix with their peers?"

"Better yet," Roger said, "they meet a variety of adults and kids of all ages— through field trips, Scouts, Little League sports, and creative activities. For example, our group takes their pets to visit the women at Safe Harbor once a month. They're widows of commercial fishermen, you know."

Qwilleran said he knew—and pulled the embroidered sampler from the tote bag. He wanted advice on having it framed. He was giving it to Polly, thinking it more suitable for her house.

The women were agog over the concept, the tiny stitches, the colors of the yarn (Siamese colors). Lisa said her next-door neighbor on the beach had a framing shop in Lockmaster. Mildred suggested a narrow molding in dark wood.

Then Arch Riker, "Did everybody hear the news about Owen Bowen? He drowned this afternoon. He'd been here only a few weeks."

There were polite murmurings: "Really too bad! . . . How old was he? . . . Where was he from? . . . Will the restaurant fold?"

Guiltily, Qwilleran thought, If he were "one of us," we'd be shocked, horrified, and ready to take up a collection for his family. But Owen was an outsider, as

182   LILIAN JACKSON BRAUN

Qwilleran himself had been before he inherited the Klingenschoen fortune and
before the *Moose County Something* was
established.

To restore the party mood Mildred
served zucchini fritters with a dill-yogurt
dip, and Qwilleran presented her with the
set of rune stones. She promised to study
the instructions and tell fortunes the next
time they met. Roger hoped the stones
would predict rain.

"It's dangerously dry. I worry about forest fires," he said. "Even the Sand Giant is
worried. People think they're hearing distant thunder, but it's really the old boy
growling in his cave."

Qwilleran, who was collecting local legends for a book to be titled *Short & Tall
Tales*, said, "Would you explain the Sand
Giant to me? I just happen to have my
tape recorder here." He knew Roger always had a yarn to tell, having been a
history teacher before switching to journalism.

"Sure!" he said, relishing an audience.
"The history of the Sand Giant goes way
back. The first explorers in this region ar-

rived by sailing ship and made camp on the beach at the base of a huge wall of sand. Strangely, they claimed to hear rumbling inside the dune, and some nights they could see a large gray shape moving among the trees on the summit. Being superstitious in those days, they decided a giant lived in a cave inside the dune. They often 'saw things' that weren't there."

"Still do," Riker muttered with a glance at Qwilleran, who nodded and chuckled.

"Through the years," Roger went on, "the Sand Giant continued to prowl and growl, and kids were afraid of being grabbed and taken to his cave if they misbehaved. His first overt act of hostility didn't occur, however, until the mid-nineteenth century, when wealthy lumbermen got the idea of building fine houses on top of the Great Dune, as it was then called. As soon as they started cutting down the ancient hardwoods, a giant sandslide engulfed the lumbercamp, killing everybody. Old-timers weren't surprised; they said the lumbermen had offended the Sand Giant. My grandparents believed that absolutely."

"My mother's forebears were believers,"

Lisa said, "but not the Campbell side of the family."

"There's more to the story," Roger went on. "For about sixty years no one tampered with the Great Dune, and Moose County prospered. Then came the economic collapse. Mines closed, and shipping went down the drain. There was no money and precious little food. But somebody got the bright idea of mining sand and shipping it Down Below to make concrete for bridges and large buildings. So the county commissioners issued a permit to hack away at the Great Dune, where Sandpit Road now cuts through. It was dangerous work because of the shifting sand, but men had to feed their families, and they kept on hacking in spite of occasional casualties.

"Eventually they tapped a pocket of hydrogen sulphide that smelled like rotten eggs and made the whole town sick. The permit was revoked, and it was back to oatmeal and turnips for hungry families . . . that is, until Prohibition came along and bootlegging was found to be profitable. There were no more sandslides, but, in certain kinds of weather, you can still hear the Sand Giant growling in his cave."

"Great story!" Qwilleran said, turning off the recorder.

"And I'm willing to believe it," said Lisa.

"Interesting," was Arch's reluctant comment.

"Dinner is served," Mildred announced. It was squash bisque, lamb stew, crusty bread, and green salad. Dessert and coffee were served on the deck, during which Qwilleran and Arch entertained them with a tell-all session about growing up in Chicago. How Qwilleran's first name was really Merlin and he'd never let any other kid use his baseball bat . . . and how Arch's nickname was Tubby and he once got sick from eating erasers . . . and how both of them were sent to the principal's office for putting glue on the teacher's chair pad.

"You did it!" said Qwilleran, pointing at his old friend.

"No, you did it, you dirty dog!"

The evening ended with laughter, and Qwilleran accompanied Lisa back along the beach.

"Do you ever see the aurora borealis?" she asked.

"Once in a while. When I first saw those dancing lights on the horizon, I was tempted to call 911."

"Have you seen many Visitors this year?"

He knew what she meant, but he hesitated. "Visitors?"

"Spacecraft," she explained. "Lyle films them, and when he gets back from Duluth, we'll have you over to look at our videos."

"Well! That's something to look forward to," he said ambiguously.

When they reached The Little Frame House, she introduced him to the Van Roops, who did picture framing.

"My shop is in Lockmaster, but we advertise in your paper," the framer said.

"Our niece knows you," his wife said. "She's a volunteer at Safe Harbor."

"Charming young woman," Qwilleran murmured.

He left the sampler at The Little Frame House, then escorted Lisa to Bah Humbug.

When he arrived at the cabin, the Siamese were waiting with the tranquillity that comes halfway between dinner and bedtime snack. It indicated that some mischief had been done. Polly's postcards, which had been stacked on the bar, were now scattered about the floor.

11

Christopher Smart's cat always greeted the morning *by wreathing his body seven times around with elegant quickness.* Qwilleran's Siamese did a few turns upon waking but never more than three, and those were done sleepily. The day after the Owen Bowen incident he fed them and addressed the two heads that bobbed over the plates of red salmon: "How come Jeoffrey did seven turns and you do only three? You have a gourmet diet and health care. He had to catch his own breakfast, and there were no vitamin drops. He never had a vaccination, blood test, or dental prophylaxis." The heads went on bobbing contentedly.

As Qwilleran thawed the last one of Doris Hawley's cinnamon rolls, it occurred to him that the closure of the backpacker case would put her back in the baking business. He telephoned, and she answered cheerily—a good sign. There were cinnamon rolls in the oven, she said.

"Save a whole pan for me," he requested. "I'll be there at midday."

In Mooseville, he picked up a basket of fresh fruit before heading for Fishport. There, the Roaring Creek was reduced to a gurgle by the lack of rain, and the Hawleys' lawn looked sadly thirsty. The burlap sack had been removed from the home-bake sign, however. He rapped on the side door, and the Doris Hawley who answered his knock was twenty years younger than the one who had recited her woes at Safe Harbor.

He presented his basket of fruit. "To celebrate the end of a nasty experience! You and Magnus handled it well."

"He's really mad! He wants to sue

somebody. I'm just glad it's over . . . but you haven't heard the latest, Mr. Q. Come in the kitchen and have a cup of tea."

The kitchen was heady with the aroma of baking ginger snaps.

"Sunday afternoon," she began, a "woman came to the door wanting to talk to the last ones who saw David alive. She was his partner, she said. She'd come from Philadelphia to claim his body and his belongings."

"What was she like?" Qwilleran asked. "I think I saw her at the hotel and walking on the beach."

Doris's description matched his. "She was kind of stiff at first but softened up when I talked about David and what a nice young man he was. He worked with computers, she said, but his hobby was UFOs, and he'd heard we had lots of sightings here."

Qwilleran huffed into his moustache at the thought of traveling that distance for such a purpose.

"She was very unhappy with the SBI and the way they questioned her. They'd taken the film from his camera and wouldn't give it to her, and they warned her not to discuss the matter—the way they did us . . . What do you think about UFOs, Mr. Q? Magnus thinks they're out there over the lake, messing with our weather somehow."

"I try to keep an open mind," he said. "I personally have seen no hard evidence, but everyone is entitled to his opinion, and I think official attempts at cover-up are a trifle absurd."

The truth was that Qwilleran was beginning to find the topic tiresome. When he returned to Mooseville, however, he found the townfolk debating another hot topic: the Owen Bowen incident. He heard about it at the bank, where he cashed a check . . . at the post office, where he found more postcards from Polly . . . at the Nasty Pasty, where he had lunch . . . at the drugstore where he bought the newspaper at two o'clock.

The druggist drew him aside. "Just between you and me, Mr. Q, I lost a good customer when Owen drowned. The guy was a boozer. Only beer and wine were served at the restaurant, but he bought a lot of liquor—and always in pints. They've got the story on page one, but not the whole story."

A news item on the front page of the *Something* read:

**M'VILLE MAN
LOST ON LAKE**

The owner of a new Mooseville restaurant was reported missing Monday, following an unexplained incident aboard his cabin cruiser. Owen Bowen, 48, proprietor of Owen's Place on Sandpit Road, sailed from the municipal pier shortly before noon. With him was his wife, Ernestine, 27, chef at the restaurant. His intention was to do some bass fishing, she said.

They anchored at a spot where the bass were said to be running and had a picnic lunch aboard, after which Bowen dropped two lines off the stern. His wife took a nap in the cabin below. She woke to find the craft rolling violently and her husband missing from the open deck.

The sheriff's marine patrol responded immediately to her call for help but found no trace of Bowen. The sheriff's helicopter continued the search until dark.

A spokesperson for the sheriff's department said, "After an exhaustive search and investigation, the conclusion is that the 25-foot craft was caught in the wake of a larger boat traveling at high speed, and Bowen was thrown off balance while tending his lines. Only a few minutes in the icy water north of the lighthouse can cause death by hypothermia."

Owen's Place, a summer operation of a Florida restaurant, will remain closed until further notice.

Qwilleran took his newspaper to the Shipwreck Tavern. He knew there would be gossip about the incident, and the tavern was the fount of controversy on such occasions. The Main Street hangout was constructed like a beached boat, and on a sunny day the interior was, by contrast, as dark as a ship's hold. He groped his way to the bar and joined an assortment of waterfront loafers.

"What for you, Mr. Q?" asked Fred, the bartender.

"Ginger ale, and also I'd like to know

how to mix a mint julep. I'm having a guest who's hooked on juleps." It was as good an excuse as any for an eavesdropping mission.

"Mint julep?" Fred muttered vaguely. "Never had a call for one. Could look it up in the barbook."

While he consulted the dogeared pages, Qwilleran tuned in:

"Always said that guy wouldn't make a go of it. He didn't belong here. Never thought he'd drown."

"You don't know he drowned. He just disappeared."

"Sheriff said he fell in."

"Nobody saw him fall in. They didn't dredge up a body."

"Maybe he jumped in for a swim and turned into an instant block of ice."

"Yep. In this lake a body goes down once and never comes up."

"I say he's down there, all right. I say he got crocked and fell overboard."

"The way I see it, the sheriff knows somethin' he ain't tellin'."

"Something he's afraid to tell! Another cover-up, like the backpacker case."

"Or like the *Jenny Lee* . . . Sing it, Fred."

"I ain't got my guitar."

"Never mind the verses. Just sing the chorus."

The bartender straightened up from studying the barbook, placed both hands squarely on the bar, and sang in a wavering country voice:

"The waves will pound, and the wind will
    blow,
And folks on this planet will never know
The honest fate of the *Jenny Lee*
And her never-forgotten crew of three."

Customers from the boats, farms, and downtown establishments applauded the oblique reference to interplanetary hocus-pocus. They nodded wisely to each other.

Meanwhile, an older man with a ruddy face and fringe of white hair around a pink bald spot slid onto the barstool next to Qwilleran. He was the head volunteer at the Shipwreck Museum. He said, "Haven't seen you at the museum this summer, Mr. Q. We have a new exhibit: photos of the petroglyphs on the Ogilvie ranch."

Qwilleran regarded him sharply. "Should I know about those?"

"Maybe not. They've been hushed up in

recent years. When they were first discovered, there was national publicity, and sightseers from all over traipsed through the pastures, stressing the sheep. Some of them even chipped off pieces for souvenirs. So Ogilvie clamped down and put a chain-link fence around the whole she-bang. But you can see very good photos at the museum."

"Interesting," said Qwilleran, who had no real interest in archaeological artifacts. "Are they like Native American pictographs?"

"Well, they're prehistoric inscriptions on stone but not pictorial—more like chicken scratching. The scientists who came up from the universities called them mathematical symbols that could be a universal language. In age they tested out to about the time of the Egyptian pyramids. Strange thing is, they were etched by some kind of technological method unknown until the twentieth century . . . Put that in your pipe and smoke it!"

Qwilleran thought, The stones could be old and the inscriptions fake. He asked, "What are they doing on the Ogilvie ranch?"

"The lake was shrunk a couple of miles.

The 'glyphs were on the lakeshore once upon a time," said the man from the museum. "During the centuries they got buried under tons of silt washed downstream. About twenty years ago we had a great flood that washed the silt away from the 'glyphs . . . You should come and see the photos, Mr. Q."

The lake air was considered salubrious, but there was also something insidious about the atmosphere that affected the brain. Everyone in Mooseville talked about interplanetary visitors, the Sand Giant, the vaporization of the *Jenny Lee*, the unexplained fate of the backpacker, the mystery of the petroglyphs, and now . . . Owen Bowen would probably become a legend. Qwilleran huffed into his moustache when he left the tavern and walked around town to work off his ire. Eventually he found himself on Sandpit Road in front of Arnold's Antiques. In the window was his rusty wheel, and in the glass-paneled door was Phreddie, standing on his hind legs and wagging his tail hospitably. Qwilleran went in.

As he expected, Arnold's first words

were, "Well, we lost our quirky neighbor. I think the place is jinxed. Do you think the Sand Giant got him? I hope I get my Waterford back. What do you think of it all, Mr. Q?"

"I don't try to fathom the mysteries of this daft community, Arnold. I just came for my wheel."

Arnold took it from the window. "I could have sold it twice, but I saved it for you."

"Sure."

"What are you planning to do with it?"

"Hang it on the wall of my cabin, over the fireplace."

"Do you need any help?"

"Thanks, but I think not. It's just a matter of hanging it from a nail, isn't it?"

"Two nails, a few inches apart."

Qwilleran said he would bring his van, which was parked behind the bank.

On the way to the bank he realized there were no nails at the cabin—or even a hammer, to his knowledge. Aunt Fanny had left him a fortune but nothing so practical as a hammer. He detoured to the hardware store. They had a revolving, four-standing bin for bulk nails, with prices posted per pound.

"Help you?" asked Cecil, surprised to see Qwilleran at the nail bin.

"Yes, I'm in the market for a couple of nails, but I'm not sure which kind."

"*Two* nails?"

"Yes, I've bought an antique wheel to hang over the fireplace."

"What kind of wheel? How large? How heavy? I'd better talk to our construction specialist. He used to build houses . . . Unc! We have a serious technical problem."

The old uncle ambled over to the bin and went into a huddle with Cecil, discussing the kind of wall, thickness of the wall, number of spokes in the wheel, and width of the wheel rim. Meanwhile Qwilleran studied a nail chart and discovered that there are almost fifteen hundred one-inch finishing nails in a pound. With some research and a little wit, he believed, he could hammer out an entertaining "Qwill Pen" column on the subject: Why is a three-inch nail called a three-penny nail? Who first said, "Thou hath hit the nail on the head?"

"How much do I owe you?" he asked when the experts had made their decision.

"No charge," said Cecil.

"That's generous of you . . . but I also need to buy a hammer."

"Lend him one," said the old man.

The two storekeepers walked to the door with their customer, and Cecil said, "Can you believe that we've lost Owen? They've got to put some speed limits on the lake and start slapping traffic tickets on irresponsible skippers."

The old man said, "If he hadn't been soaked to the gills, it wouldn'ta happened."

Qwilleran asked, "How is his wife?" Does anyone know?"

"She's better off without that horse's tail," the old man said.

In a flash, an idea struck Qwilleran. As if hit on the head with a hammer, he virtually saw stars! . . . *Koko knew about Owen's death before and after the fact!* Else, why his sudden interest in *A Horse's Tail*? The connection between a book title (that Koko couldn't read) and an epithet bestowed on Owen Bowen (that Koko hadn't heard) would seem far-fetched to anyone but Qwilleran, who had witnessed the cat's semantic associations before. Though Koko's communications were coincidental in the extreme, they always proved to be accurate! Sometimes prophetic!

Then Qwilleran had second thoughts: Could he be succumbing to Mooseville Madness? Everyone around here was over the top! He had to get out!

12

Hanging the four-foot wheel over the fireplace, twelve feet above the floor, was no easy task, and Qwilleran tackled it Wednesday morning when he was fresh. (Koko also was fresh and meddlesome.) First, the eight-foot stepladder had to be maneuvered from the toolshed on a narrow path between a dense growth of wild cherry bushes, then into the small screened kitchen porch and the cabin.

Yum Yum ducked under the sofa and was not seen during the rest of the operation; Koko inspected every inch of the ladder for hidden hazards; Qwilleran sat down and had a cup of coffee. So far, so good.

Next, Koko took his post on the mantel and watched the man struggle up the ladder with the large round object, propping it precariously on the horizontal timber before going down for a pencil, two nails, and the borrowed hammer. At this point, the cat's sniffing of the rusty wheel became so fervent that he was banished to the porch, and Qwilleran had another cup of coffee.

That done, he climbed up the ladder again, eyeballed the space, penciled two dots, hammered the nails into the wall fairly straight, and hung the wheel. While up there, he noticed a crack in the top surface of the mantel, a square-cut, handhewn timber that spanned the width of the room. The old logs and timbers occasionally cracked in the middle of the night, sounding like pistol shots. It was never a serious split—only a fine crevice. A hundred years of such cracks actually added character to the interior. The one on the mantel was just wide enough for wedging postcards upright. More than a dozen had come from Canada, each with Polly's hur-

riedly scrawled message on the back. Together they made a pictorial frieze several
feet long.

She and her sister had seen four plays:
Oedipus Rex, Macbeth, Major Barbara,
and *The Importance of Being Earnest.* The
cards pictured a grotesque mask used in
Greek drama . . . the classic sketch of
Shakespeare with pointed beard and re-
ceding hairline . . . a portrait of George
Bernard Shaw . . . and the Toulouse-
Lautrec caricature of Oscar Wilde.

Other cards had been mailed as they
motored east: Niagra Falls from the Canadian side: a tower almost half a mile high
with a restaurant at the top; Parliament
buildings; a ship going through the locks; a
mountain lodge; two cathedrals; an ox-
drawn hay wagon; an aerial view of small
islands; and more. Before weekend there
would be views of a quaint fishing village
and a rocky island blanketed with resting
waterfowl.

As soon as Qwilleran opened the porch
door, Koko bounded in to see the exhibit,
walking behind the upstanding cards in a
space too narrow for any but a sure-
footed, long-legged Siamese. Next he

stood on his hind legs and stretched to paw the rim of the rusty wheel.

"NO!" Qwilleran thundered. Koko winced and returned to the postcards, sniffing each like a connoisseur of fine wines. The cat seemed to be looking for something. He finally gave his seal of approval, a gentle fang mark, to the two cards that were third and fourth from the left end of the row: portraits of the two Irish playwrights. Qwilleran thought, That cat! Now he's getting interested in dramaturgy!

At the Northern Lights Hotel, where Qwilleran went for another cup of coffee and some scuttlebutt, he was stopped in the lobby by Wayne Stacy. The hotelkeeper said, "Qwill! Just the guy I want to see! I have a favor to ask."

"Shoot! But I reserve the right to dodge."

"I think you'll like it. Saturday we have the annual dogcart races sponsored by the chamber of commerce for the last thirty years. Wetherby Goode usually announces them, but this year he's got a conflict—wedding, or something like that. Could you help us out?"

"What does it entail?"

"You just announce each race, name the winners in each class, and hand out the trophies. Somebody will be at your elbow, supplying the information. I guess anybody could do it, but you've got the voice for it."

Qwilleran appreciated compliments on his vocal quality. "What time on Saturday?"

"First gun at eleven A.M. Come early and have breakfast with us."

"Okay. It'll look good on my resumé," Qwilleran said. "And now tell me: How's Mrs. Bowen?"

"To tell the truth, I haven't seen her. She has her meals sent up to her. But last night she ordered dinner for two and some champagne!"

"A promising sign."

"That's what we thought. The chamber hopes the restaurant will reopen—and soon."

Qwilleran thought, Who was up there helping her drink the champagne? Derek? If so, did Elizabeth know? She was quite possessive.

Qwilleran changed his mind about having a cup of hotel coffee and hustled to Elizabeth's Magic.

Derek was there, working on the space for the new lending library. Barb Ogilvie was there, too, arranging a window display of her handknits.

Elizabeth said, "Qwill, you should buy one of Barb's lovely vests for Polly as a welcome-home gift. They're unique. I'm sure she'd like a white one with sculptured surface texture. When is she due to return?"

"I pick her up at the airport Monday."

"Barb could do a custom design for you . . . Barb! Conference, please!" To Qwilleran she whispered, "She's not herself today. Something's wrong. A special order might perk her up."

He agreed that the flippant, flamboyant ex-balloon-chaser with mischievous eyes was looking subdued.

Elizabeth took charge of the conference. She explained that Qwilleran's friend was returning from a long vacation on Monday, and he wanted a very special gift for her. She was a woman with excellent taste and would be thrilled with a Barb Ogilvie original. Her size was fourteen. She said, "Why don't you drop everything, Barb? Go home and start the needles flying. I'll finish the window for you."

"I'll see what I can do," said the knitter, and after some aimless puttering, she left and drove away in her pickup.

Qwilleran thought, She's argued with Alice about smoking . . . or she's having man-trouble again . . . or she's received an upsetting letter from Florida.

Elizabeth, on the other hand, was elated. "We've had some good news," she said. "Ernie called this morning and asked Derek to take her some recipe books from the RV parked behind the restaurant. She wants to open next Tuesday—with a whole new menu, except that skewered potatoes will still be featured at lunchtime. Why don't you buy some skewers, Qwill? I know you don't cook, but Polly will enjoy using them when she comes up on weekends, and they're decorative when hung on the kitchen wall. They're handmade, you know, by Mike Zander, who did your copper sailboat. I suggest a group of five for the best effect. The fingergrips have five motifs: fish, bird, shell, boat, and tree, designed to hang on brads."

Qwilleran was fascinated by his protégée's transformation from a shy, bewildered young woman to a forceful and successful businesswoman—and a weaver of spells when it came to selling merchandise.

"Whatever you say," he agreed. "But I've just finished the complicated task of buying two nails at Huggins Hardware and borrowing a hammer. I don't know how they'll feel about selling five brads."

"You're a dear, Qwill," she said. "I'll give you five, and you can borrow one of Derek's hammers."

Qwilleran went to the crooked door and saw Derek ripping out the hairdresser's plumbing fixtures. "You have an abundance of skills, young man."

"Hi, Mr. Q! Come in and grab a pipe wrench."

"No, thanks. I prefer to cheer from the sidelines."

"I'm trying to finish this job for Liz before the restaurant opens Tuesday. Some people will say it's too soon, but Ernie says people will rally around while the tragedy is fresh in their minds. If you delay, they cool off."

"Frankly, I'm glad to have you back in business. Save me a table for two Tuesday night . . . How much more work do you have to do here?"

"Me? Just paint the pink walls in a kind of nothing color. The tile will be covered with carpet. The shelves are on order. The books have been shipped from Chicago. Liz inherited them from her dad, you know." Derek put down his wrench and approached Qwilleran in a confidential manner. "Ernie needs some cash flow. That's why we're opening next week, and she wants to sell the boat. I wish you'd have a look at it. Maybe you know somebody interested in a good cash deal."

"Where is the boat?"

"Near the marina office, with a for sale sign in the windshield. It's the *Suncatcher*."

"*Suncatcher*?" Qwilleran stroked his moustache with sudden interest.

"Yeah. You'd think Owen would call it *Bottoms Up!*"

Clutching his package of skewers and one of Derek's hammers, Qwilleran walked briskly to the marina, and there was the *Suncatcher*, gleaming white in the sun. Whether it was the one that had trafficked with *Fast Mama* was hard to tell. All cabin cruisers looked alike to a confirmed landlubber, and the name was a common one.

Its pristine whiteness was marred only by a faint stain on the deck—very faint— about the size of a spilled glass of red wine. One of the white waterproof seat cushions appeared to be missing, and an eagle eye could detect a few tiny spots on the transom. Otherwise it seemed to be shipshape.

What interested Qwilleran was: Whether or not it had been involved with *Fast Mama*, and why. He also wondered about the speedboat's home port. He had a sudden impulse to drive to the resort town of Brrr, several miles to the east.

Brrr was the coldest spot in the county in winter and the breeziest in summer. Built on a promontory with an excellent harbor, it had the famous Hotel Booze on its summit, a historic landmark for boaters and fishermen. Now the hotel was owned by Gary Pratt, whose Black Bear Café served the county's best burger.

Gary was behind the bar when Qwilleran slid cautiously onto a rickety barstool. The shabbiness of the café was one of its attractions. Another was the mounted black bear at the entrance. Still another was the owner himself, whose shaggy hairiness and shambling gait gave him an ursine persona.

"Is it too late to get a bearburger?" Qwilleran asked him.

"Never too late for you, Qwill, even if I have to grill it myself. And while you're waiting, how about a slug of that poison you drink?"

As Gary disappeared into the kitchen and Qwilleran poured a bottle of Squunk water into a glass of ice cubes, a man on a nearby barstool said, "Good stuff you're drinkin', mister. Been drinkin' it all my life."

"Seems to agree with you," Qwilleran said. The other customer, though white-haired and wrinkled, spoke briskly and sat with a straight spine.

"Yep. Just had my ninetieth birthday."

"Do you expect me to believe that?" Qwilleran said jovially.

The advocate of Squunk water moved closer and flashed his driver's license for proof. "I was ten years old when my grand-paw discovered the stuff you're drinkin'."

Qwilleran sensed another story for *Short & Tall Tales*. "Mind if I tape this conversation? I'm Jim Qwilleran with the *Moose County Something*."

A bony hand shot forward. "Haley Babcock. Land surveyor, retired."

They shook hands—the man had a firm grip—and the recorder was placed on the bar between them. "Where did Squunk water get its name, Mr. Babcock?"

"Well, now . . . my grandpaw's farm was rocky pastureland, good for sheep and goats, but not a tree or shrub in sight! Grandmaw always wished she had a nice shady porch for sittin' and knittin'. One day Grandpaw came home from livestock market with some green twigs wrapped in wet paper. He'd paid a Canadian feller a dollar for 'em—big money in those days. It was called Squunkberry vine and supposed to be fast-growin' and healthy for livestock."

Gary brought the bearburger and said, "Glad you guys got together. Haley's got a good yarn for your book, Qwill."

"Did the green twigs do the trick?" Qwilleran asked.

"Yep. They grew a foot overnight! With big green leaves! In two weeks the vine covered the whole porch and started creepin' over the roof. Grandpaw cut it back, but the dang stuff crept across the yard, over the dog kennels, over the outhouse, over the fences. The whole family had to fight it every day with axes. Couldn't stop it!"

"Sounds like a Hitchcock movie," Qwilleran said. "How about the livestock? Couldn't they help keep it under control?"

"That's the joke! They wouldn't touch it! You'd think it was poison. Come winter, it died down, and Grandpaw hoped the snow and ice would freeze it out. No luck! In spring, it started up again. There was a big ditch out in front, and it filled the whole ditch. Then one day Grandpaw thought he heard bubblin' and gurglin' in the ditch. He put a pipe down and pumped up good clean water! The folks at the county tested it, and it was full of healthy minerals. Neighbors came from all over with jugs to fill up . . . free."

"When did they start selling it?"

"Well, now . . . after Grandpaw died, my uncles defaulted on taxes, and the farm went to the county. They leased it to a bottlin' company."

"And the vines are still growing?"

"Yep. But they've got big equipment to control 'em." Mr. Babcock asked for his tab and reached in his pocket.

"My treat!" Qwilleran insisted. "And thank you for a great story." He and Gary watched as the old man walked away with a vigorous stride. "Hope I function that way when I'm ninety," Qwilleran said.

"Wish I functioned that good right now! Want another Squunk water?"

"Yep, as our friend would say. Although I suspect Mr. Babcock is a shill to help you sell more of it . . . Now tell me the local reaction to the Owen Bowen incident."

"What you'd expect: irresponsible skipper with fast boat, endangering smaller craft. Was the guy an experienced boater?"

"One presumes so. He brought his own boat up from Florida."

"Will the restaurant fold? I could use another cook for the summer."

"The chef is out of your class, Gary. You couldn't even read her menu without a Larousse."

"Are you kidding? I don't even know what a Larousse is!"

Qwilleran remarked casually. "John Bushland has a new boat."

"Yeah, he docked here and had lunch one day. Funny, isn't it, that he doesn't get married again—good-looking guy with a successful business."

"What is really funny, Gary, is how you new bridegrooms want everyone else to jump off the bridge. Does misery love company—or what?"

"You sound like sour grapes. Did Polly give you the gate? I haven't seen her lately."

"She's vacationing in Canada with her sister."

"Uh-huh . . . sure."

And so it went, until Qwilleran said, "Speaking of our friend Bushy, he took me for a cruise on his new boat, and we saw a grungy speedboat that aroused our curiosity. It was called *Fast Mama*. Have you seen it in these waters?"

"Can't say that I have, and it's the kind of name I'd notice. Around here we name our boats *Happy Days* or *Sweet Iva May* . . . Is it important, Qwill? I'll phone down to the marina." He ambled to the phone and soon ambled back again. "The name doesn't ring anybody's bell down at the pier. If you ask me, it sounds like a boat from Bixby County. Their taste is raunchier than ours."

"I don't know anything about Bixby, except that they have a button club, and our office manager is a member."

"There's a lot more to Bixby than button-collecting," Gary said. "It's chiefly industrial and big on sports, but they're troubled with unemployment, poor schools, a high drop-out rate, and all that."

The barkeeper wandered off to serve a trio of boaters at the other end of the bar, and Qwilleran thought, If the *Suncatcher* involved with *Fast Mama* is the one from Florida, what was Owen's game? . . . and how did he make his connection? . . . and was the speedboat again in the vicinity on the day he disappeared? . . . and did Ernie notice it? . . . and could Owen have been abducted while she was sleeping off a wine jag below deck? . . . and if so, was Owen murdered?

These were questions to discuss with Andrew Brodie over a nightcap at Qwilleran's Pickax address, and the sooner the better. The Siamese would be glad to return to their spacious home in a converted barn. Furthermore, there was a good neighbor there who catered home-cooked meals for the three of them. They had been at the beach for more than two weeks. There was no real need to stay longer.

Driving away from the Black Bear Café, Qwilleran made his plans. This was Wednesday. He could move his household back to Pickax on Thursday, then drive to the shore briefly on Saturday morning to announce the dogcart races. On Monday he would pick up Polly at the airport, and Tuesday evening they would celebrate at the opening night of Owen's Place.

It was neat planning, but Robert Burns was right; the best-laid plans go off-line.

13

When Qwilleran arrived at the cabin after his visit to the Black Bear Café, he found a cardboard carton on the doorstep, apparently delivered by someone from the newspaper. It contained bundles of postcards in response to his column on Lisa's great-grandmother's diary. Enthusiasm for the witty journalist who lectured in Pickax circa 1895 had been handed down in many local families.

Indoors, the Siamese were lounging on the coffee table in a shaft of sunlight that slanted down from a window, their fur glistening. Qwilleran took a moment to admire them. "You are two gorgeous brutes!" Yum Yum lowered her head modestly. Koko, who was keeping the Mark Twain reference book warm, stared with meaningful intensity.

Qwilleran patted his moustache as an idea crept into his consciousness. On an impulse he phoned Hixie Rice, a promotion director for the *Moose County Something*.

"Hixie! I've just thought of a sensational idea to promote the city of Pickax—and the newspaper, too, if we care to sponsor it."

"Is it as big as the Great Food Explo? She asked dubiously.

"Bigger."

"As big as the Ice Festival?"

"Bigger, and guaranteed not to melt. How about meeting me for lunch tomorrow? I'd suggest Owen's Place, but you know what happened."

"How about Linguini's? They still have the same menu, the same mom-and-pop operation, the same dull color scheme, and the same broken locks on the restrooms. But the food is wonderful!"

"You might also bring Fran Brodie, if she's available on short notice."

"We'll be there, I promise," Hixie said.

"You've got me all pumped up. Can you give me a clue?"

"No," he said.

Not surprisingly—after thawing some pork barbecue for his dinner—Qwilleran had a graphic dream Wednesday night: He was having lunch with Mark Twain at an unidentified restaurant. The man across the table was the same one who appeared on the jacket of Koko's favorite book: white three-piece suit, cravat with diamond stickpin, good head of hair, high forehead, alert brows, rampant moustache. He was genial and talkative as they compared notes. One was born Samuel Langhorne Clemens, in Florida; the other was born Merlin James Qwilleran, in Chicago. They discussed journalism, travel, cats, lecturing—and then the picture faded, and Qwilleran was lying in his dark bed in the cabin.

The dream was a portent of an eventful day. After breakfast, the cats wanted to play rough-and-tumble, and Qwilleran obliged by whipping an old paisley necktie through the air and watched them leap, grab, collide, and roll over on the floor. Like Montaigne, whose cat liked to play with a garter, he was not sure who enjoyed it more—the cats or himself.

Next he hung the skewers, pounding five brads in a row in the log wall above the kitchen counter. Koko immediately sniffed the fingergrips and touched the thin twisted skewers with a nervous paw. "Stay away from those," Qwilleran warned him. "They're for skewering potatoes, not members of the family."

His morning's work was finished quickly. The "Qwill Pen" for Friday was a reader-participation stunt, meaning that unsuspecting readers did the legwork for him. In June, he had posed a burning question, and hundreds of subscribers had mailed their replies on postcards, which were then tabulated by the office manager. Qwilleran had only to incorporate the results into his entertaining prose. The question: Why do your cats squeeze their eyes? Eight thoughtful explanations were submitted, the most popular being: "They're smiling."

Shortly before noon he set out for his lunch date carrying his canvas tote bag from the Pickax library. At the restaurant outside the town of Brrr he was greeted by Mrs. Linguini, who recognized his mous-

tache. "Ah! Mr. Grape Juice! No wine! . . .
Poppa!" she shouted toward the kitchen.
"Mr. Grape Juice here!"

Mr. Linguini came rushing to shake
hands, his right hand damp from the
steam of boiling pasta, then rushed back
to the kitchen.

"Sit anywhere," said his wife with a
grand gesture. "You want grape juice?"

"Wait till my guests arrive," he said. "I
think they'll want some of your good red
wine." It was commonly believed that
Poppa Linguini made his own wine in the
basement; also, someone was growing
wine grapes on a rocky slope outside
Brrr—where the days were sunny and
nights were cool—and it was most certainly Mr. Linguini.

Qwilleran took a table for four and
propped the canvas tote bag on the fourth
chair.

Soon his guests bustled in excitedly,
saying, "There he is! . . . He's always
early . . . Qwill, you look wonderful! . . .
Your vacation agrees with you!"

Standing to pull out their chairs, he responded with a frown: "I haven't had a
minute's rest since coming to the beach! I

do more loafing in Pickax . . . You two look as if you'd won the lottery!"

"We're excited about your secret project!" Hixie explained.

"We've been making wild guesses all the way up here," Fran added.

In Qwilleran's opinion they were the two most glamorous women in the county—in personality, dress, and grooming. The publicity woman was always recklessly vivacious; the interior designer was always coolly dynamic.

"First, some wine!" he proposed. It was immediately served in squat tumblers, with grape juice for the host. He said, "You'd be drinking imported pinot noir from thin-stemmed wine glasses, if Owen's Place hadn't closed."

"I feel bad about that. I really do," said Hixie. "When the Bowens first arrived, I called on him to set up an ad campaign for the summer. He didn't have much personality, but he was incredibly handsome and rather conceited—what locals call uppity."

"Do you know exactly what happened to him?" Fran asked Qwilleran.

"Only what I read in the paper."

Roguishly, Hixie said, "I think he was

leaning over the rail, admiring his reflection in the surface of the lake, and he fell in."

"That's an uncharitable thought," Qwilleran rebuked her, "but possibly true. The good news is that Owen's Place will reopen next Tuesday evening with Derek as manager."

"He can't work that weekend!" Fran objected. "It's the last week of our play, and he has the title role!"

"I'll be glad to sub for him at the restaurant," Hixie volunteered. She had managed the Old Stone Mill before joining the *Something*. "He was our busboy at the Mill. It's good to see him making progress."

"Onward and especially upward," Fran added.

Qwilleran told them how Derek had introduced skewered potatoes as a luncheon dish, deskewering them at tableside with the dramatic flourish of a Cyrano de Bergerac.

"More wine!" he called to Mrs. Linguini, "And then we'll order." After selections were made, he presented his proposition:

"Moose County has never been associated with a prominent literary figure. No local boy ever made good as a famous writer. So I suggest we adopt one and observe his birthday, just as the men's lodge observes Robert Burns Night on January 25. I've had tremendous reader response to my column about Lisa Compton's great-grandmother's diary. She was a Mark Twain fan in the nineteenth century and as goofy, in a Victorian way, as an Elvis fan in the mid-twentieth. Mark Twain made Pickax one of his stops on a lecture tour, and the locals flocked to hear him speak, bought his books, wrote letters about him, and made entries in their journals. He had a fantastic way with audiences of that era. He was a journalist, a humorist, and a prolific creative writer . . . So I propose an annual Mark Twain celebration to honor an American icon who never passed this way again."

Hixie's eyes were shining as she thought of the possibilities. "How far do we want to go?"

"We could easily fill a week with special events. Proceeds could go to the county's literacy program. Samuel Langhorne Clemens would approve of that."

Fran said, "The theater club could do readings from his books or dramatizations from *Tom Sawyer* and *Huckleberry Finn.*"

"We could have a parade—with floats!" Hixie said ecstatically. "That would draw the TV crews from Down Below."

"We could stage a banquet. Does anyone know what he liked to eat?"

"How about a lecture by some university bigwig from Down Below?"

"Why not rename a street Mark Twain Boulevard?"

"The *Something* could offer an annual Mark Twain scholarship to a student going into journalism."

Then Qwilleran suggested, "When the renovated hotel opens in September, perhaps we could name one room after him and hang a large portrait." He unsheathed *Mark Twain A to Z* from the canvas tote bag, displaying the splendid photograph on the book jacket.

Hixie squealed with delight. "We could have a Mark Twain Look-Alike Contest, and Qwill would win!"

"You'd never get him into a three-piece suit," Fran said.

"Their eyes are different. Their brows are different."

"Qwill is handsomer."

"And sexier."

He huffed into his moustache. "Here comes the nutrimento."

Mrs. Linguini came from the kitchen, balancing three plates. She banged one down in front of Fran, saying, "Stuffed manicotti . . . Very good!" The next landed in front of Hixie. "Veal marsala . . . Very good!" Qwilleran got the third. "Lasagna . . . The best!"

After the frenzied brainstorming, they enjoyed lunch quietly with only desultory conversation.

Qwilleran mentioned that Owen's widow was anxious to sell their boat and might consider any offer of cash.

Fran announced that the next play at the barn theater would be *Life with Father*, and they were looking for five kids with red hair—to save the cost of wigs.

Hixie said she was stuck with fifteen thousand large lapel buttons in a polar bear design, rendered useless when the Ice Festival thawed out. She wondered if they could be returned to the manufacturer and reworked for another purpose.

Qwilleran confided that he might work on a scenario for a film in collaboration with a corvidologist—not to be confused with a cardiologist.

Then Fran shocked them with the news (confidential, of course) that Amanda Goodwinter was quitting the city council and running for mayor. Qwilleran said he would campaign for her.

Finally, Hixie said she had seen proof-sheets of the first "Ask Ms. Gramma" column and had brought a set with her. "I want to know what you both think of it," she said. "I think she wrote it with a pitcher of martinis on her desk."

At her suggestion, Qwilleran read it aloud at the table:

Dear sweet readers . . . Ms. Gramma was thrilled to pieces by your response to last week's announcement. It shows you really care about saying it right. Stick around, and we'll have some fun, too. Ms. Gramma loves to step on toes and upset applecarts. For starters, here's a note from a brave guy who dares to challenge Ms. Gramma's grammar.

Dear Ms. Gramma . . . You goofed. "Say it right" is wrong. It should be "say it correctly."—Bill, in Black Creek.

Dear Billy Boy . . . "Right" can be an adverb or an adjective. Look it up in your dictionary, sweetheart.

Dear Ms. Gramma . . . My husband and two grown sons are educated and know better, but they still insist on saying "he don't" instead of "he doesn't." What to do?—Pauline, in Pickax.

Dear Pauline . . . Some men think "he don't" is macho. Give up, my dear. The male animal is as stubborn as a mule— and we all know about mules, don't we?

Fran interrupted. "Who's writing this column?"

"Only Junior Goodwinter knows, and he's not telling," said Hixie.

"Well, I think it's a man."

"I do, too," said Qwilleran. "I also think it's not very good."

"Read some more," Hixie urged.

Dear Ms. Gramma . . . When I was in school, we had a campaign against the word "ain't." If anyone used it, the whole

class yelled "oink oink." It worked!—Isabelle, in Trawnto.

Dear Isabelle . . . Ms. Gramma here-
by gives permission to her readers to
yell "oink oink" whenever they hear
"ain't" in a public place. Thanks for the
idea, honey. Ms. Gramma is not respon-
sible, however, for physical assault or
verbal obscenities resulting from the
oinking.

Dear Ms. Gramma . . . Some People
who are fussy about their speech say
"between you and I" instead of "between you and me." Why?—Linda in
Mooseville.

Dear Linda . . . For the same reason
they crook their pinky when drinking
tea. They think it's correct, but it ain't . . .
Oops! Sorry! . . . Ms. Gramma could
write a volume about pronouns following prepositions, honey, but it would be
boring, so let's do it the easy way. All together now . . . *Between you and me!*

When Qwilleran had concluded the
reading, he asked, "Do you think it was
written by a staffer or a free lancer? Or a
committee?"

"I won't rest until I find out," Hixie said.

"Don't waste your time on Ms. Gramma," Qwilleran told her. "Apply your brain to a Mark Twain celebration."

Satisfied with the events of the lunch hour and looking forward to a return to Pickax, Qwilleran planned his exodus while driving back to Mooseville. There was no need to close the cabin completely. With Polly back in town they would be spending weekends at the beach, entertaining other couples with cocktails on the porch and dinner at Owen's Place. The Siamese would stay in their luxurious barn with a cat-sitter.

Near Top o' the Dunes he bought a frozen dinner at a roadside convenience store and started watching for the old stone chimney. He hoped it would never succumb to the bulldozers of a Roadside Improvement Coalition; he had developed an affection for the grotesque monolith. When he spotted the historic landmark in the distance, he also saw a vehicle turning into the K driveway. It was yellow! It was a school bus!

Qwilleran was indignant. He resented

trespassers, and he was not fond of schoolchildren en masse. Individually, he found them amusing—the McBee boy and Celia Robinson's grandson, for example. But what were they doing on his property without permission? School had let out in mid-June, but school buses were used for all kinds of summer enrichment activities.

Arriving at his driveway, he pursued the bus, noting a flash of yellow as it lumbered over the dunes and between the trees. His van bounced recklessly in its wake. Even so, the bus was already in the clearing when Qwilleran drove up and parked directly behind it; there would be no escape without due explanation! He jumped from the driver's seat, expecting to see a yardful of noisy kids racing around and alarming the cats. The only sign of life was a tall, broad-shouldered figure at the top of the sandladder, gazing at the lake. Qwilleran noted a farmer's straw hat, jeans, field boots, and some kind of inscription on the back of the T-shirt.

"Hello, there!" he shouted with a note of annoyance.

The uninvited guest turned, revealing a life-size crow on the T-shirt. "You must be Qwill," she said in a clear authoritative voice. "I'm Tess, Joe Bunker's cousin."

"Oh! . . . If I'd known you were coming, I'd have been here to welcome you," he said, tactfully mixing rebuke with apology. "Joe said you'd phone me from Horseradish when you arrived."

"I changed my itinerary. Hope you don't mind."

"Not at all," he said crisply. He disliked being taken by surprise. "Go on the porch and make yourself comfortable while I unlock the cabin and put my purchases in the freezer."

Only then did he realize that the yellow vehicle, a mini-bus, was boldly labeled RE-PUBLIC OF CROWMANIA. So was the back of her T-shirt.

Indoors he briefed the Siamese. "We have company. She's out on the porch. She's a corvidologist, but harmless. Don't sniff her boots; it's considered impolite."

When he opened the door to the lake porch, they hung back warily. Tess was sitting with her legs crossed and her hat off, her dark hair sleeked back into a bun. Her features were clean-cut, with thin lips and high cheekbones. "You have a lot of crows on the beach," she said. "I'm glad I brought a supply of dried corn."

"How far have you traveled today?" he asked.

"Not far. Just from my aunt's house in Bixby. I tried calling you from there, and when there was no answer, I decided to take a chance and come anyway."

"Would you explain your bus?"

"I'd love to! It's used for field trips with students and for dissemination of information at all other times—propaganda, if you will. As Joe may have told you, I believe crows are the next big craze, following pigs, frogs, owls, monkeys, whales, and dinosaurs. The crow is a noble bird—intelligent, rather handsome, well organized, cooperative, and very focused. A flock knows where it's going and flies directly there. 'Straight as the crow flies' is no accidental cliché. As for the crow's voice, it's authoritative, with an extensive vocabulary far beyond the common 'caw.' What's your reaction to crows, Qwill?"

"They all look alike."

"On the contrary, they have different

personalities, physiques, and body language, as you'll see when you read the literature I've brought you. Why don't we bring in my luggage, and I'll unpack, and then we'll talk some more."

Luggage? Wetherby had said nothing about her coming as a houseguest!

"Joe tells me you don't cook. I'd be glad to prepare meals while I'm here."

Meals? How long does she think she's staying? Qwilleran asked himself.

"Just tell me what you like to eat," she said. "I make a fantastic macaroni-and-cheese with horseradish, if you like that sort of thing."

"First, let's bring your luggage in," he said.

There were two enormous duffel bags and a briefcase in the bus. Together they carried them through the woods to the guest house.

"It's small, but it has indoor plumbing," he said. "We call it the Snuggery."

"It's cute!" she said. "I love it!"

Qwilleran rushed back to the cabin to make his first mint julep and slapped his forehead in dismay. No mint! He had

plenty of bourbon but no fresh mint. The
Rikers grew it in their backyard, and Mildred had said he could help himself at
any time. He grabbed his car keys and
drove to Top o' the Dunes, left the motor
running, and grabbed a handful of what
he presumed was mint. It smelled like
mint. Then he drove recklessly back to
the cabin and arrived just as Tess was
coming through the woods in a fresh
denim shirt.

"How would you like a mint julep?" he
asked.

"Oh, I love mint juleps!" she exclaimed.
"But the doctor won't let me have anything stronger than wine. What are you
drinking?"

"Ginger ale."

"Then I'll have the same. This is a
charming cabin. How old is it?" She wandered about, admiring the stone fireplace,
the copper sailboat, the Mark Twain collection. She commented on the row of postcards. "There are two on the floor!"

"They probably have fang marks in the
corners," Qwilleran said. "Just put them on
the coffee table. I'll replace them."

He had a hunch which two they would be: George Bernard Shaw with his handsome beard . . . and Oscar Wilde with a posy in his buttonhole.

14

Qwilleran took his houseguest to dinner at the Northern Lights Hotel, apologizing for the ordinary menu. "We would have dined with class at Owen's Place, but Owen had the misfortune to drown. The cook here has been a fixture for thirty years, and he cooks plain."

They ordered Swiss steak, and to take their minds off the gravy thick as wallpaper paste, and the overboiled carrots, and the potatoes whipped to the consistency of shaving cream, Qwilleran asked a leading question: "What was it like to grow up in Horseradish?"

"Actually, by the time I was born," she said, "agriculture had given away to tourism. We were no longer the horseradish capital of the Middle West, but lingering fumes from the former industry still make an invigorating atmosphere for vacationers."

"But were your forebears horseradish farmers?"

"No, they were in shipping. Our town was the chief port for all of Lockmaster County, and my great-grandfather's adventures as captain of the sailing vessel *Princess* have made him a legendary figure. You see, all sorts of commodities were being shipped in and out. There was still some gold-mining in the interior, as well as a thriving fur trade, especially beaver. This made cargo ships prey to buccaneers. Did you know there were pirates on the lakes at one time?"

"Joe told me that their victims were often made to walk the plank. He never mentioned the *Princess*."

"Oh, she was famous in her day! On one occasion the *Princess* sailed out of harbor with a cargo and had just lost sight of land when a craft with a black flag loomed on the horizon. Captain Bunker gave some unusual orders: When the pirate ship hove to, the crew would go below with crowbars and wet rags."

Tess paused to observe her listener's reaction; she had told this tale many times.

"A volley was fired across the bow of the *Princess*, and she dropped sail. Then all hands disappeared into the hold, which was stowed with kegs of grated horseradish mixed with vinegar. The pirates came aboard, stomping and cursing. Where was the blankety-blank crew? It was a blankety-blank ghost ship! They stormed down the hatch . . . Immediately the lids came off the kegs, and the fumes rose like poison gas! The pirates choked and staggered blindly, while the crew—masked with wet rags—threw handfuls of the stuff and swung their crowbars. Overpowered, the pirates were dragged to the deck and heaved overboard."

"Tess! That's a fascinating story!" Qwilleran exclaimed. "Would you mind repeating it when my tape recorder is handy? I'm collecting local legends for a book."

"I'd love to! The pirate story is true, but there are many Bunyanesque tales about our town, like the cargo ship powered by horseradish fumes before steam boilers came into use."

Qwilleran found her well read, well spoken, and not a bad-looking dinner date. He was glad she had not worn her crow T-shirt. They discussed cats (she had two) and journalism (the ethics of responsibility) but not a word about crows. Yet, the sooner the crow-show was off the docket, the sooner he could take off for Pickax. For breakfast they would have coffee and rolls and then spend the morning talking crow, after which he would hope to see the taillights of the yellow bus disappearing down the driveway.

To direct the conversation accordingly, he asked, "Do you plan to sell T-shirts as a tie-in with the film?"

"Eventually," she said. "Meanwhile, I've brought one for you. What size do you wear? They're cut full."

"Uh . . . large," he said vaguely, as he tried to imagine himself with a crow on his chest. "Do you have any real assurance that your film will be produced?"

"Definitely! The university has the technology and the artists and the grant. My responsibility is to provide the scenario. I see the film as being entertaining, educational, and inspirational—with the crows solving problems, overcoming evil, and respecting the environment and family values."

For a moment, it crossed Qwilleran's mind that the crow-show was another of Wetherby Goode's practical jokes, like his Intergalactic System of Managed Weather that would control temperature, regulate precipitation, harness winds, eliminate natural disasters, and promote global amity. One never knew whether he was prankster or visionary.

Tess was saying, "The bus attracts attention wherever I go, and I'm always happy to tell strangers about *Corvus americanus.* They're curious to know how crows function in their cooperative families of seven: a breeding pair and five adult helpers."

"So am I," Qwilleran said.

"I left a dossier on your bar—papers I've written for scientific journals—and you can read them tomorrow while I run into town. Do you have a market that sells good meat? I know this is lamb country, and one

244 LILIAN JACKSON BRAUN

of my specialties is lamb shank with beans, lumberjack style."

That was another of Qwilleran's absolute favorites. Okay, he thought; she can stay a second night. He said, "Grott's Grocery is run by four generations: Gramps, Pop, Sonny, and Kiddo. They still cut meat to order and cheese from the wheel. Anything you buy can go on my charge account. Tell Gramps you're my guest."

Then a surge of hospitality prompted him to say, "Would you like to see a play at the barn theater tomorrow night? It's a sellout, but they reserve a few passes for visiting celebrities."

"I love barn theater!" she said.

Tess retired early to the Snuggery—she wanted to do some reading—and Qwilleran phoned Wetherby Goode in Indian Village. He said, "Guess who drove a school bus into my yard today and moved into the guest house! Your cousin!"

"That woman! She was supposed to go to the family homestead in Horseradish and phone you from there."

"Well, she changed her mind."

"What do you think of her, Qwill?"

"She's as nutty as you are! But pleasant and interesting. Did you tell her that I have a weakness for macaroni-and-cheese and lamb shank?"

"No. I never mentioned food. I swear!"

"The problem is, she seems to like it here, but I've got to move back to Pickax."

"Throw her out! She won't mind," Wetherby said. "And thanks, Qwill, for pinch hitting for me at the dogcart races Saturday."

Friday morning Qwilleran served a continental breakfast on the kitchen porch, which was flooded with morning sun. He reconstituted frozen orange juice, thawed cinnamon rolls, and pressed the button on the automated coffeemaker. The Siamese joined them, looking for warm concrete on which to sun. Koko stretched out full-length to do his grooming in solarized comfort.

"He's a ham," Qwilleran explained. "He likes an audience for his morning ablutions. An eighteenth-century poet described the ritual in ten steps: *For first he looks upon his forepaws to see if they are clean. For secondly, he kicks up behind to clear away there."*

Tess laughed heartily and said, "*For thirdly he works it upon stretch, with his forepaws extended."*

"You know Christopher Smart!" Qwilleran said in pleased surprise.

"Oh, I adored Christopher Smart! I named my male cat after Jeoffrey. Stop and think: For two centuries—or two millennia—cats have been washing up in the same simple, efficient way, while we go on inventing revolutionary improvements that may or may not be successful or even necessary."

"Avoid radical theories in Mooseville," he advised. "Don't get yourself arrested. The local lawmen may consider the Republic of Crowmania subversive . . . Incidentally, while you're there, be sure to visit Elizabeth's Magic on Oak Street."

After the yellow bus had wheeled down the driveway, Qwilleran took the file of crow literature to the lake porch and read it carefully, hoping to find something—anything—that would suggest a scenario to

Tess's specifications. He was disappointed. There was nothing that made crows seem glamorous or heroic or inspirational. They had some repulsive feeding habits. They could be nasty to other species or even other crows who happened to be outside their family cooperative. They enjoyed pulling the tails of dogs, sheep, and birds of a different feather. Some of their hobbies bordered on the kinky, like encouraging ants to run through their feathers.

"*Please!*" he said in repugnance.

He thought about the friendly family of seven who visited the beach daily and amused the Siamese. They cawed, and Koko cawed right back. They strutted. They showed off. They seemed to have innocent fun.

Now, in the cold light of research, crows seemed snobbish, antisocial, prejudiced, and nauseous in some relationships. Qwilleran threw the dossier aside and drove into Mooseville to buy red wine and fruit juices for sangria—and to see if Tess had been arrested. He found the yellow bus on the hotel parking lot surrounded by excited tourists. Tess, in her crow T-shirt, stood on the bottom step of the bus and answered questions. A patrol car cruised slowly past the scene.

As he listened to her captivating her audience, Wayne Stacy came up to him. "She's a friend of yours? She asked permission to park on the lot and said she was visiting you."

"She's Wetherby's cousin from Down Below. She's here to visit her family in Horseradish."

"I told her she could park there for an hour. Anything that pleases the tourists is good for business. But after that we have to clear the lot and paint lines on the asphalt for the dogcart event—lanes for racers, you know. We use a temporary kind of marker and then hope it won't rain tonight and wash it away. A big storm is expected, coming down from Canada, but Wetherby says it isn't due till Sunday. He appreciates your filling in for him, Qwill, and so do we."

There was a ripple of applause around the bus as the crowd started to dissolve, and Qwilleran moved away before Tess could see him. According to schedule, it was time for her to go home and start cooking the lamb. He went to Elizabeth's Magic to inquire about his special order.

"Barb assured me she'll finish it on time," Elizabeth said. "And thank you, Qwill, for sending me that delightful Dr. Bunker. She loved everything in my shop and bought several things: goofy socks for her cousin and her cat-sitter, skewers for herself, and a Thai caftan for her grandmother in Horseradish, who's celebrating her hundredth birthday."

"Did she talk about crows?"

"Enthusiastically! We discussed the possibilities for crow-oriented souvenirs. I said I would relax my rule against T-shirts and would be willing to sell one like hers if the proceeds went to scientific research."

"Good for you!"

"Come and see a new item that a friend of yours brought in—Janelle Van Roop."

"Oh?" What else could he say?

In the craft section there was a display of small stuffed creatures called Kalico Kittens and made of rosebud-patterned cotton. Eight inches long including tail, they were primitive but appealing, having splayed legs, a spike of a tail, and oversized ears. Eyes, whiskers, and tiny mouth were embroidered, not too carefully.

Elizabeth said, "Their lopsided features make them amusing and rather lovable, don't you think? Dr. Bunker called them contemporary folk art and bought several for gifts."

"Who makes them?"

"The elderly ladies at Safe Harbor. I'm handling them without commission. It was my idea to give each kitten a name—nothing cute or faddy but traditional and dignified—like Clarence, Martha, Spencer, Agatha, and so on. Why don't you buy one for the cats?"

He knew they would be quickly vetoed by the Siamese, who ignored velvet mice, rubber frogs, and tinkling plastic balls. They preferred a necktie with a man on the other end . . . "Okay," he said, "I'll take this one. Gertrude."

Tess would be returning to the cabin to prepare dinner—she knew where to find the key—and Qwilleran intended to stay out of sight lest he be asked to peel potatoes. He sat on the hotel veranda to read Friday's paper and consider the crow scenario. He was definitely cooling off. The question was: How to break the news to Tess? She was a nice woman—the cousin of a good friend. If he reneged, it should be done with grace: a few ideas, a little advice, a lot of encouragement.

He would conclude the matter after the play. Then she could leave after breakfast, and he could return to Pickax after the dogcart races.

All went well that evening: Qwilleran thought the lamb shank superb; Tess loved the play. Afterward, he served sangria on the lake porch and said, "Tess, your visit has been memorable! I only wish I could work on your project. Unfortunately, I have other commitments. But I can visualize the possibilities—and the problems—and the decisions to be made."

"I understand," she said, with less disappointment than he had anticipated. "What kind of decisions do you mean?"

"In regard to the plot: Who or what will provide the conflict? Other species of birds? Other wildlife? Humans? Mechanical equipment? Scarecrows? . . . First of all, will it be an all-bird cast? I would think not. Crows seem to hang around cow pastures; do they have any relationships with cattle other than scatological? Who are the crows' friends, and who are their foes?"

Tess asked, "What about dialogue? How anthropomorphic do we want to get?"

"Well . . . you might have all the animals in the cast speak in their own voices—with a human voice-over translating their caws and clucks and woofs."

"What language do you suppose scarecrows speak?"

Qwilleran said, "That's one for the language department at your university." He smoothed his moustache as an idea began to form. "The scarecrow's job is to protect the crops from the crows—right? Suppose he makes friends with the crows and starts an underground movement in their behalf. His collaboration is discovered, and he's condemned to death. If he's made a sympathetic character, this could be a highly emotional situation."

Tess said, "I'm getting the weeps already."

They discussed names for the characters. The breeding pair could be Queen Croquette and her consort Prince Chromosome.

"I love it! I love it!" she cried.

"May I refresh your drink, Tess?"

It was a happy corvidologist who took the electric lantern and found her way to the Snuggery. Before saying goodnight, she said, "Do you realize you have thimbleberries behind the toolshed? I could pick some and make thimbleberry pancakes for breakfast."

"Splendid idea!" Qwilleran said.

"And Grott's Grocery had some beautiful rib-eye steaks. I bought two, thinking we could have steak au poivre tomorrow night—with skewered potatoes." Before Qwilleran could react, she said, "Do you realize one of the skewers is missing? There were five."

15

After the thimbleberry pancakes, Tess took the yellow bus to the unsuspecting town of Brrr to propagandize for the Republic of Crowmania. Qwilleran drove to Mooseville for the dogcart races. Traffic was unusually heavy on the lakeshore road. Even before he reached the city limits he saw cars, vans, and pickups parked in farmyards, as well as on both shoulders of the road. Droves of pedestrians were walking toward downtown, where three blocks were blockaded. Only racing units and the cars of officials were admitted. Qwilleran showed his press card and was told to park in the marina lot.

He had never seen so many kids in one place: clamoring for attention; shrieking for joy; crying; jumping up and down; getting lost; tussling. Adults, who were in the minority, had tots in arms, toddlers in strollers, and infants in backpacks. Both hotel lots were cleared for official use: one marked as a racetrack, the other serving as a paddock.

Wayne Stacy spotted Qwilleran and explained the system. Forty youngsters would ride in forty toy wagons hitched to forty family pets. There were boxers, retrievers, hounds, pit bulls, terriers, huskies, German shepherds, and one giant schnauzer, and plenty of mongrels, all classified according to weight. The young drivers had numbers on their backs; the dogs wore boleros in the family's racing colors. One adult accompanied each racing unit in the paddock; a second adult member of the family would stand at the finish line.

Over the years the event had become a carnival. Wagons were decorated with paint or crepe paper, and the young drivers were in costume. There were astronauts, ballerinas, red devils, pirates, cowboys and girls, clowns, and black cats mingling with the forty dogs, eighty adults, and numerous harassed officials.

Qwilleran said, "It looks like absolute chaos, but I suppose you've done it before."

"We sure have! For thirty years," said Stacy. "Some of the young parents were once racers themselves."

"Isn't it somewhat hazardous?"

"We've never lost a kid or a dog, knock on wood."

"Well, I wish you'd explain the procedure."

"Okay. There are preliminaries, and there are finals. You announce the names and numbers of racers in each heat. Five units come from the paddock and line up. The whistle blows, and they're off! Moms and dads wait at the finish line, cheering their dog on."

"How do I know who's who and what's what?" Qwilleran shouted above the general noise.

"Cecil Huggins will hand you the information. At the end, you present two trophies—Class A and Class B. There'll be picture-taking."

"What are the trophies?"

"Inscribed mugs. Plus, every kid in the race gets an ice-cream cone and a little something to take home. Every dog gets a bone."

"Do I present the bones?"

The two men had been shouting in each other's ears, and when Qwilleran went to the mike, even his amplified voice could hardly be heard above the din. It doubled in decibel level when the first whistle blew.

Spectators cheered their favorites and screamed at unexpected happenings. Once, a basset hound left the track in mid-course and trotted to the sidelines for some sociability . . . Another time, two dogs who were neck-and-neck in the race started to fight and dumped their drivers . . . And then the giant schnauzer crossed the finish line and kept on going down Main Street, while the driver screamed and parents and officials ran in pursuit.

Through it all, Qwilleran gritted his teeth and did his job.

The grand champion in Class B was a

yellowish, brownish mongrel in a denim bolero, with a four-year-old cowgirl at the reins.

"They've been training," Qwilleran said to Cecil.

"All year long! They're serious about this race."

In Class A the champion was a black Labrador in a red, white, and blue bolero, with a seven-year-old astronaut for a driver.

Qwilleran said to the astronaut's father, "Aren't you with the Scotten Fisheries? I met you when I was doing a story on commercial fisheries. I'm Jim Qwilleran."

"Right! I'm Phil Scotten. You went out with us, hauling nets. You wrote a good article."

"Thanks. It was a priceless experience . . . Nice dog you've got."

"Right! Einstein is a retired G-dog, trained to do drug search. Very intelligent. He's what they call a passive searcher. When he detects somethin', he just sits down."

"Is that so?" Qwilleran patted his moustache as a whimsical idea occurred to him. He considered it further as he walked down to the waterfront parking lot, where racing units were being loaded into pickups.

He approached the Einstein team and said, "I just had a crazy idea. There's a boat over here that I'm thinking of buying. Would Einstein give it a sniff?"

"Sure. He'd probably enjoy it."

The two men and the dog walked over to the *Suncatcher* and went aboard. Einstein gave a passing sniff at the stain on the deck and the dark spots on the transom, but it was the cabin that interested him. They took him below. He inspected everything—and sat down.

"I think he's tired," said the fisherman. "He's gettin' on in years, and he's had a hard day."

Driving back to the cabin, Qwilleran pounded his moustache with his fist. Now he had something pertinent to discuss with Brodie: first, the rendezvous of the *Suncatcher* and *Fast Mama*; then Owen's disappearance; then Einstein's behavior.

As for his houseguest, if she failed to leave on Sunday morning, he was prepared to throw her out, as Wetherby had suggested. Still, he would prefer to use psychology. For example, he could drop some leading remarks into the conversation at dinner.

During the cocktail hour: "I certainly enjoyed our visit, Tess!"

With the soup course (she had promised gazpacho): "I hope you've found this trip worthwhile."

With the steak: "Feel free to phone me about any future developments in Crowmania, such as a civil war or military coup."

With the dessert: "They're expecting violent weather, starting tomorrow noon."

With the coffee: "How long does it take to drive to Horseradish?"

The excellent dinner was served on the porch, and Qwilleran dropped his hints as planned. Afterward, he said, "I'll clean up the kitchen, in case there's something you'd like to do." (Like packing, he thought.)

"Thanks," she said. "I'd like to phone my cat-sitter. The last time we talked, Princess was acting strangely."

"She misses you," Qwilleran was quick to say. "The females especially are upset by a long absence."

Since the phone was on the bar, he could hardly avoid hearing her conversation: "Hi, Sandy. It's me again. How's Princess? . . . Is she still coughing? . . . Give her one of those pills. Mix it with her food, and let's hope she keeps it down . . . Tell Jeoffrey not to stress her . . . No, I don't know when I'll be home. I'm busy making friends for the Republic. But I'll keep in touch."

Qwilleran had yet another idea. He said to his guest, "Before you leave, I want to tape your story about Captain Bunker and the pirates. *Why don't we do it right now?*" He made it sound urgent.

"I'd love to tell it again!" she said. "But first I want to feed my friends on the beach." She had been scattering dried corn once or twice a day, and the family of seven who had entertained Koko was now an extended family of forty or more.

Then, still immune to Qwilleran's dropped hints, she said, "Do you realize that Grott's Grocery carries duck eggs? I couldn't resist buying four for breakfast. We'll have mushroom omelettes. I also bought some of their delicious Cheddar for

macaroni and cheese. I'll prepare a casserole after breakfast, and we'll have it for
lunch."

She had touched the two most vulnera-
ble spots in his considerable appetite. De-
feated, he mumbled, "Sounds good," and
proceeded to rationalize: Actors need audiences, writers need readers, and cooks
need mouths to feed.

"Yow!" said Koko.

"He talks more than Jeoffrey does," she
said.

"Koko is a communicator." They were
sitting on the lake porch, waiting for the
purple martins to swoop in for their evening ballet, during which each bird would
consume his weight in mosquitoes, according to conventional wisdom. Yum Yum
was on a nearby chair with Gertrude. Koko
was on his pedestal. "He's a very smart
cat," Qwilleran went on. "That's because I
read aloud to them. Yum Yum goes to
sleep, but Koko listens, and his brain ab-
sorbs meanings even if his ears don't
know words."

"Thought transference," she said. "But
how does he communicate?"

"He finds a way. His senses are incredible. He knows when the phone is going to ring. A couple of weeks ago he knew there was a dead body buried in beach sand near here, and he led me to it."

Tess said, "All cats are prescient to some extent. They're aware of an approaching storm, or even an earthquake. Have you had any studies made of Koko's capabilities?"

"No! I don't want any studies, any publicity. This conversation is between you and me . . . Do I have your word?"

"Absolutely! And when I get home I'm going to start reading to Jeoffrey and Princess."

16

On Sunday morning the sun was shining despite the weather warnings, and Tess came from the Snuggery in shorts, sandals, and a different type of crow T-shirt, depicting three nest-builders.

"Everyone out of the kitchen!" she ordered cheerily. "The poor man's Julia Child is about to perform miracles . . . By the way," she added as she picked up a skewer from the countertop, "one of these skewers keeps falling off its nail."

"It's no accident," Qwilleran said. "Koko thinks it's a toy. It was a mistake to hang them there . . . Is there anything I can do for you?"

"You might scatter some corn on the beach."

"There are no crows today," he protested.

"Scatter it, and they will come."

She was right. They came out of the woods in a black cloud. Qwilleran got out of their way and back to the lake porch to wait for the omelettes. The sky was Alice blue (one of Polly's favorite colors) and the lake was dazzlingly bright. Surely there was no imminent storm. From the kitchen came aromas of melting butter, brewing coffee, sautéeing mushrooms, and toasting muffins. With great feelings of satisfaction, he refigured his reunion with Polly.

She would be pleased with her new vest and would undoubtedly bring him something from Canada: a piece of Inuit sculpture or a CD of French-Canadian jazz. At Owen's Place she would be delighted to see Derek in a position of responsibility; she had long been convinced of his potential. Arch's reluctant membership in the knitting club would amuse her, and she would want to know all about the parade, Bushy's new boat, and the embroidered sampler from Safe Harbor. She would be dismayed by Owen's unpopularity and shocked by his *lacustrine* disappearance. (Good word; Polly would like it.)

He would avoid mention of the *Suncatcher* and *Fast Mama*; it alarmed her when he took on self-assigned investigations.

When breakfast was served, Qwilleran paraphrased Dickens. "There never was such an omelette!"

"Thank you," Tess said. "In all modesty, I admit that I make the world's best, although it's said that a cook who makes a perfect omelette can't make anything else. What do you think of the duck eggs? They're rich, because ducks are amphibious and high in fat content."

"Why do they figure so prominently in American slang?" he asked. "We have lame ducks, dead ducks, and sitting ducks."

"Slang is full of edibles," she said. "We call someone a meatball; the boss is the big cheese; something easy is a piece of cake—"

"Or duck soup."

* * *

After breakfast, when Tess was assembling the promised casserole, Qwilleran went into town for the *New York Times* and sat on the hotel veranda for a while— to read a little, eavesdrop, and watch the harbor activity. He had a view of the marina office and was somewhat surprised to see a sheriff's deputy and a state trooper looking at the *Suncatcher*. If Einstein's owner had tipped off the authorities about the dog's behavior, that was good! The police had been dragging their feet, in Qwilleran's opinion. If an investigation would implicate Ernie in wrongdoing, that was bad! He saw her through Derek's worshipful eyes; he himself admired her cuisine, and he was inclined to empathize with anyone who was not "one of us."

Qwilleran returned to the cabin and found Tess on the porch, reading about ravens. He asked, "Do they really say 'nevermore' or was that Poe-etic license?"

"For a pun as bad as that," she retorted, "you have to pay a forfeit."

"Will you settle for a glass of sangria?"

"I'd love it! And while you're in the

kitchen, would you turn on the oven to pre-
heat? Set it at three-fifty."

Eventually the casserole went into the
oven to bake for forty minutes, and what
happened in that brief time was a farce
worthy of Feydeau—fast-moving, comic,
improbable—and best described by Qwilleran's own notes in his personal journal:

Sunday, June 14
Beautiful day, although storm predicted. Cats apprehensive.
At 1:15 Tess and I are on the lake
porch drinking sangria and cranberry
juice, respectively. The cats are huddled in a corner. Suddenly they're
alerted. Someone's approaching on
the beach. A young woman in shorts
and sunglasses is carrying a large flat
package. She starts up our sandladder. I go out to investigate. In a lazy
drawl with breathy pauses she says,
"Hi, Mr. Q. I brought . . . your sampler.
My uncle . . . framed it." I'm Janelle
from Safe Harbor!
At 1:25 she's on the porch, being introduced to Tess. I go to get her a glass
of sangria. While in the kitchen I see a
red pickup pulling in, and out steps Barb

Ogilvie in shorts and sunglasses, carrying another flat package. "I brought your vest," she says moodily. "Elizabeth said you had to have it today." I offer her a glass of sangria and take her around to the porch to meet the others.

At 1:30 I mix another batch of sangria, while Tess tells them about an old doctor who treated all ailments alike—with a horseradish diet, horseradish poultices, and horseradish inhalants. His patients never died; they just evaporated.

At 1:35 I hear a tooting behind the cabin. It's an airport rental car, and out steps Polly! In shock, I say, "Your plane isn't due till tomorrow!" She says sweetly, "I couldn't wait to get home. I flew in on my broomstick." I take her around to the porch and introduce her to the three young women. She's somewhat surprised.

At 1:40 Tess takes the casserole out of the oven. I'm wondering if there's enough to serve five.

At 1:45 the sun disappears behind cloud cover, and all the dark glasses come off. Barb looks terrible without them; she's been crying.

At 1:50 the phone rings. I answer, and a man shouts, "Where is she?

Where is that woman?" I say calmly, "I have four here. Which one do you want?" It's Wetherby. Tess is supposed to be in Horseradish as guest of honor at a family reunion. Fifty relatives have come from all over to meet the Bunkers' first Ph.D. Photographers are there from two newspapers. I return to the porch and tell Tess, "It's for you." As she rushes to the phone, she's saying, "Oh, no! Oh, no!"

At 1:55 she returns to the porch, wide-eyed. "I've got to leave! I'm going to pack! There's a car blocking the drive!" It's the rental car, and I offer to move it, but Polly wants to go home to see Brutus and Catta.

At 2:00 Polly leaves, saying she'll phone me.

At 2:05 Tess leaves in a confusion of embarrassment and remorse. I tell her to drive carefully.

At 2:10 Janelle leaves because it looks like rain.

At 2:15 Barb leaves, looking more troubled than ever. I ask if something's wrong. She nods, but says she can't talk about it.

At 2:20 they're all gone, and I have a

chance to look at the framing job on my sampler (neat) and Polly's hand-knitted vest (sensational).

At 2:25 the sky turns yellowish-gray. There's a strange whistling in the tops of the pines. Eerie! Koko goes into a tizzy, racing around, knocking things down, scattering stuff. I tell him, "Christopher Smart's cat would never wreck the house. He was a paragon of virtue. *For he will not do destruction, if he is well fed.*" He wriggles as if tired of hearing about Jeoffrey.

At 2:30 I close the windows of guesthouse and van and stack the furniture on the north porch. The storm is coming from Canada.

At 2:35 it's really dark. Lights have to be turned on. All the windows and doors are closed, and I sit down to wait for the storm to hit. But where are the cats? Nowhere in sight! Where's the macaroni and cheese? I yell "Koko!" From the pantry comes a yargle—half yowl and half swallow. The two of them are on the counter, with their heads down and tails up. They're devouring the cheese, horseradish and all, but avoiding the macaroni.

The wind and rain that bombarded the shoreline communities on Sunday afternoon was a true squall—brief but violent. In five minutes the lake surface went from glassy to raging surf. Wind-lashed rain slammed into the north side of the cabin, rattling the window glass, seeping under the door and around the window frames. Qwilleran was kept busy soaking up the flood with towels and wringing them out in a pail. Then the blow ended as abruptly as it had started. Although heavy rain continued to fall, it fell in vertical sheets instead of horizontal waves. There was damage indoors but only as a result of Koko's tizzy: crumpled rugs, a toppled table lamp, books and papers on the floor, and several yards of paper towels unrolled in the kitchen.

The good news was that the power had not failed, and the telephone still had a dial tone. He called Polly. "Just checking to see if you got home safely."

"Luckily I was indoors before the onslaught. Now it's merely a normal rainfall, steady but not destructive. How about you?"

"We're getting a thorough drenching, but the worst is over. Were the cats glad to see you?" he asked.

"Catta was. She's too young to know she's supposed to boycott me for twenty-four hours after a prolonged absence."

"Well, you're probably tired and have things to do."

"I admit I'm exhausted."

"Make a cup of tea and have a Lorna Doone," he advised, knowing her choice of pick-me-up. "And let me know tomorrow if there's anything I can do. You'll need groceries, and I expect to be back in Pickax tomorrow morning as soon as it stops raining."

He hung up and started rectifying Koko's rearrangement of the cabin interior. Patiently he rerolled the paper toweling, straightened the rugs, put the lamp together again, and restored two postcards to their proper place.

The gully-washer, as the locals called such a storm, continued all night, pounding the cabin roof and alarming the cats. They were used to the lofty roof of the barn in Pickax; in the tiny cabin, the weather was too close for comfort. Qwilleran allowed Yum Yum to crawl under his bedclothes, and eventually brave Koko followed.

* * * *

On Monday morning it was still raining steadily, and roads outside Mooseville were flooded. Qwilleran would have to stay at the cabin one more day. The interior was dismal, even with all the lights turned on, and the cats were moping.

"Count your blessings," he told them. "It could be worse."

Nevertheless they huddled on the floor, facing each other, in their bored-stiff pose. (Reading aloud to them was no good because of the noise of the rain on the roof.) Only then did Qwilleran remember the Kalico Kat. He found it in a drawer and placed it on the floor between their dispirited noses.

Koko stretched his neck to sniff it and then withdrew into his torpor. Qwilleran thought, So much for contemporary American folk art. Yum Yum, on the other hand, showed some signs of interest.

"This is Gertrude," Qwilleran said. "She's come to live with you."

Murmuring strangely, she crept forward and sniffed the toy thoroughly, then gave it a few licks. Her maternal instincts were aroused. Closing her mouth over the scruff of the toy's neck, she carried it to her favorite corner on the sofa. She had adopted Gertrude.

It was a bright spot in a dull day, and it inspired Qwilleran to telephone the florist in downtown Pickax. He recognized the silky voice of Claudine, a gentle young person with innocent blue eyes. "Good morning," he said. "Is it raining cats and dogs where you are?"

"This sounds like Mr. Q," she said. "Where are you calling from?"

"The haunts of coot and hern."

"Oh, Mr. Q, I never know when you're serious and when you're kidding."

"Have your new flowers come in, or are you still selling last week's wilted stock?"

"You're awful! They're unloading the express truck right now. What would you like?"

"A mixed bouquet for Polly, to be delivered to Indian Village ASAP."

"I hope she isn't sick."

"She's suffering from post-vacation letdown, and I want the flowers to get there while she still feels rotten."

"Our van doesn't go to Indian Village till noon."

"Too late. Send the flowers by taxi, and put it on my bill."

"What do you want the card to say?"

"Just 'the grocer boy.' No name." When Claudine hesitated, he spelled it for her.

"Oh! The *grocer boy*! You're always pulling a fast one, Mr. Q."

"Don't hang up," he said. "I also want to send a large bouquet to a restaurant in Mooseville tomorrow. The roads should be open by then. It's Owen's Place on Sandpit Road, and it's decorated in white, pink, and yellow. Just say 'from a well-wisher' on the card. And make it something special; it's an upscale establishment."

Within an hour Qwilleran received a phone call, and a woman's cheery voice said, "Is this the grocer boy? I'd like a dozen oranges."

"With or without seeds?" he replied.

"Qwill, dear, the flowers are lovely. Thank you so much! They came by taxi! It's so good to be home."

"I must say I was shocked to see you yesterday."

"I was shocked to see that aggregation of youthful pulchritude on your porch—in shorts and sunglasses—and drinking! I won't ask you to explain."

"Good! And I won't ask you about the charming and erudite professor who talked you into spending more time in Quebec City."

"We'll have much news to exchange tomorrow night, dear. Is it still raining at the beach?"

"It's pouring! Everything in the cabin is damp: my clothes, the sofas, the cats' fur, my books! The one I've been reading is so soggy, I've retitled it *A Damp Yankee in King Arthur's Court* . . . See you tomorrow."

As the morning splashed on, Qwilleran found himself going rain-crazy, unable to concentrate on either reading or writing. It was the roar! Like Niagara without the picture postcards. So far there were no leaks in the roof, but dryness was all the cabin had to offer. The cats were playing Yin and Yang on the sofa, their ears buried in each other's fur. Should he thaw a second-rate burger for lunch? Or venture into the outside world at the risk of being drowned? He could get an equally second-rate burger at the hotel.

Holding a waterproof jacket over his head, Qwilleran dashed for his van and headed for Mooseville. There were few vehicles on the highway, and they were moving cautiously as the drivers peered through windshields made opaque by the hurtling rain. There was not yet any flooding; the sandy terrain drained well, but how much more could it take? Already the ditches were beginning to look like canals.

In town, there were many parked cars, but everyone was indoors. He found them in the hotel lobby and coffee shop—gloomy vacationers, looking stranded and bored. Some sat on the veranda and watched the raindrops hitting the pavement hard enough to splash vertically like a million tiny geysers.

Wayne Stacy was relatively cheerful when he saw Qwilleran. "How about that? It held off till after the races! The C of C will have to send a fifth of something to the weatherman. And we got the new storm sewers just in time, thanks to the K Fund. The stupid voters turned down millage three times before we applied for a grant."

"Perhaps they're not so stupid," Qwilleran observed. "I hope the downpour stops in time for the opening of Owen's Place."

"Even if it does, how many diners will venture out? They said on the radio that the access roads are flooded . . . Are you here for lunch? Be our guest!"

After lunch, Qwilleran made a wet dash to the hardware store for batteries, since a soaking rain usually caused trees to topple.

Cecil Huggins said, "We've sold out of camp stoves and bottled water. Grott's has sold out of bread and milk. Folks are expecting the worst. Another worry is a rising lake level and beach erosion."

"If every raindrop is big enough to fill a shot glass," Qwilleran said, "how many shots of rain are needed to raise the level of a twenty-thousand-square-mile lake by one inch?"

Cecil's great-uncle was pessimistic. "When the Sand Giant gets mad, he gets mad! And he's mad at somethin' or somebody."

From there, Qwilleran went to Elizabeth's Magic, knowing there was always someone there on a Monday, come hell or high water. He parked at the curb, facing the wrong way, and made a dash for the overhang. When he hammered on the door, Derek came from the rear to let him in.

"Hi, Mr. Q! What d'you think of this rain?"

"The Sand Giant was sick of hearing complaints about the dry summer."

"Come in the back and have coffee. I've been sorting books, and I'm ready for a break."

They sat in the spidery chairs, and Qwilleran asked, "Where's Elizabeth?"

"On Grand Island for her brother's birthday. They picked her up yesterday in the family yacht—the *Argonaut*. Maybe you've seen it in the harbor. Her dad was into Latin and Greek and all that stuff. He taught Liz the Greek alphabet. Do you know anyone who can recite the Greek alphabet?"

"Not in Moose County."

"She's teaching me. Alpha, beta, gamma, delta . . . that's as far as I've got."

Qwilleran fingered his moustache; there were some answered questions here. "These books of his that she's putting into her lending library . . . I trust they're not in Greek and Latin."

Derek laughed—nervously, it appeared. "No, nothing like that."

"No one has mentioned what the old boy collected. Don't tell me it's pornography, and Liz is opening an adult lending library in downtown Mooseville!"

There was another nervous negative.

"Come on, Derek. Am I supposed to play Twenty Questions? What's to stop me from going to the stockroom and having a look around?"

"Okay, but promise you won't tell Liz I spilled the beans . . . Her dad had everything that was ever printed about UFOs—in all languages. He had *Chariots of the Gods* in the original German."

Qwilleran huffed into his moustache. "And why was she keeping it a secret?"

"Well, you know how you are about UFOs—you and Arch Riker. After the publicity breaks in the Chicago papers and on the TV networks, she thinks you'll break down and give the story coverage."

"And you expect that kind of national attention?"

"Well, the PR department at the K Fund is handling it, and they've been up here collecting facts. You see, it's not just a tourist gimmick. It'll attract serious researchers. The valuable books will be available only to scholars."

Qwilleran huffed into his moustache again.

Pleadingly, Derek said, "Promise me you won't say anything about this. If you do, I'll be in bad trouble."

"I promise. But one question: Who's going to catalogue the books?"

"Her dad had them all catalogued."

"I see . . . Well, I'd better get home and see if the cabin has floated away. I hear your play was rained out last night. How about the restaurant tomorrow? Access roads are flooded."

"I know. I talked to Ernie on the phone, but she's determined to open . . . Wait a second, Qwill, and I'll give you a printout of the new menu."

17

Still it rained. Returning to the cabin on Monday afternoon, Qwilleran found two reproachful cats huddled on the coffee table, giving him an accusing eye, and two postcards on the floor.

"I don't like it any more than you do," he said. "Think dry thoughts, and maybe it'll stop."

It was mid-afternoon in July but dark as twilight in January. He turned on all the lights and flopped on the sofa with the new menu from Owen's Place. Reading it from Polly's viewpoint, he guessed that her appetizer would be the miniature acorn squash roasted with a stuffing of wild rice, fresh corn, and caramelized onion. Her entrée would probably be the potato-crusted filet of salmon served with shiitake mushrooms, saffron risotto, and chive beurre blanc.

The telephone rang, making all three of them jump, and a grouchy male voice said, "I've been trying to reach you all afternoon. Where've you been?"

"To the haunts of coot and hern," Qwilleran retorted. He and Arch Riker had a lifetime license to be rude to each other.

"This rain's driving me nuts! If only it would turn off for five minutes and start again, I wouldn't care, but it's relentless! Mildred copes by cooking. Why don't you come and eat with us?"

"What's on the menu?"

"Gumbo. And she's made some kind of pie. Come anytime, I'm mixing a martini for myself right now."

Qwilleran changed his shirt, fed the cats, and steered the van between the raindrops to Top o' the Dune.

Mildred met him at the kitchen door. "You're so brave, Qwill, to come out in this downpour!"

"I'll do anything for a free meal, especially if you prepared it. What kind of pie did you make?"

"A new recipe. Strawberry lemon cream. Arch is in the living room with his cocktail. Shall I do something creative with tomato juice for you?"

"Please. And don't forget the hot sauce."

"He's as cross as a bear. See if you can cheer him up."

Qwilleran found him growling at the TV screen and said playfully, "Don't bother to get up, Arch."

"I didn't intend to," his friend grumbled.

"If you want me to stay, you'll have to turn off the boob tube. I brought a copy of the new menu at Owen's Place."

"I'm dying to know what they offer," said Mildred.

"Okay. How's this for an appetizer? Grilled petite tenderloins of venison with smoked bacon, braised cabbage strudel, and a sun-dried Bing cherry demiglaze?"

"Ridiculous!" Arch said. "Give me the traditional dishes that Millie cooks."

"Traditional, with a dollop of love thrown in," she corrected.

"Speaking of food, I've had a live-in

cook for a few days," Qwilleran said, pausing long enough to enjoy Arch's astonishment. Then he told them about Wetherby's cousin and her crow proposal.

"Don't take on any fringe projects," Arch objected petulantly. "If you haven't enough to do, we'll run the 'Qwill Pen' three times a week. The subscribers are howling for it."

"Let them howl!"

Qwilleran had never seen Arch so argumentative, but then he had never seen a rain storm so annoying.

The gumbo was filled with the good things that Mildred kept in her larder: chicken, shrimp, sausage—plus rice, vegetables, and spices.

During the dessert, Arch said, "If you want to hear something absurd, Junior has received some leaked information about a library of UFO literature opening in Mooseville! Can you believe that?"

"Sure. It's a popular subject on the shore, with everyone but you and me," said Qwilleran. "Even Lyle Compton watches for flying saucers with a telescope."

"Lyle's a fool!"

Mildred said firmly, "He's an intelligent, educated, sophisticated individual." Turning to Arch, she said, "That makes me a fool, too."

"I didn't say that!" her husband snapped.

"You implied it!"

"I'm going to bed! I haven't slept a wink all day!" Arch stomped out of the room.

Mildred said softly, "He's hardheaded, isn't he? I don't dare mention the rune stones you gave me, Qwill. They're similar to tarot cards, in that the reader has to bring certain instincts to the interpretation."

"Hmmm," Qwilleran murmured. Foretelling the future by any method was outside his frame of belief.

Looking deeply concerned, she said, "The stones say we're headed for disaster. One has to assume it's connected with the unnatural volume of water that's being dumped on us all at once. I really believe we should move back to Indian Village, but how do I convince Arch? He loves it here—when it isn't raining. You and the cats should move back to Pickax also, Qwill."

"We intend to. Now that Polly's home and going back to work Wednesday, she'll need help with grocery shopping. She's been gone a month. Her cupboard must be bare."

"Qwill, I don't know why you and Polly don't get married. You have strong feelings for her, and I know she adores you!"

"It wouldn't work," he explained. "She's a tea-drinker, and I'm a coffee-drinker, and there are certain basics that must be considered."

While driving back to the cabin through the persistent rain, Qwilleran thought about Mildred's eccentric interest in the occult and compared it with his own belief in Koko's prescient talents. The cat knew when the phone was about to ring and when a storm was brewing. Now Mildred had predicted a disaster for the area. Whimsically, Qwilleran imagined Koko pulling the luggage out of the closet and searching the bookshelves for Stevenson's *Travels with a Donkey*. That would be no more far-fetched than the cat's sudden interest in *A Horse's Tale* when Owen Bowen disappeared. And how about the backpacker? Not only did Koko sense that the body was buried in the sandhill, but he managed to lead Qwilleran to the site. And how to explain the cat's obsession with the postcards? Qwilleran reviewed what he knew about the two men pictured. Shaw was a playwright, music critic, socialist, Nobel prize winner, and antivivisectionist; Wilde was a novelist, poet, playwright, and aesthete.

"Wait a minute!" he shouted at the steering wheel. "What's wrong with me?" He took a chance on driving faster and dashed into the cabin without bothering to cover his head. The two cards were on the floor as usual. Why had he not thought to turn them over? He had not read Polly's messages since they arrived two weeks before!

"We have tickets for *Major Barbara* tonight—not my favorite Shaw play, but it will be beautifully done."

"A male actor plays Lady Bracknell in *The Importance of Being Earnest*. Always a delightful comedy."

Qwilleran felt a crawling sensation on his upper lip as the scrawled message brought to mind Barb Ogilvie and Ernestine Bowen. It was pure coincidence, and yet . . . He looked at Koko.

"Yow!" said the cat, squeezing his eyes.

Qwilleran asked himself, Did the two women know each other in Florida? Did Barb work in the Bowens' restaurant? Was Owen the "older man" who entered Barb's life when she was feeling low? She claimed to have moved back north to avoid trouble.

Previously, she may have extolled Moose County as a summer paradise. Did Owen respond to the chamber of commerce ad because of the climate, or because of the seductive young woman? And what was Ernie's reaction to the move? There the conjectures became tangled. Did she know of the affair—or not? Were her objections overruled? There was more intrigue in this situation than met the eye. Answers might explain Barb's depression in the days following Owen's disappearance.

Qwilleran was in deep contemplation when the telephone rang.

It was Tess, calling from Horseradish. "I hear you're having rain there," she said.

"A few sprinkles."

"Sorry to leave so abruptly yesterday. I was having such a wonderful time. Thank you, Qwill, for your hospitality and the

clever ideas for the scenario. I left a T-shirt
for you on the dresser in the Snuggery; let
me know if it's the wrong size. And by the
way, I told Jeoffrey and Princess about
your cats' elitist diet, and now they don't
want to eat cat food."

"Likely story," Qwilleran said. "How was
the family reunion?"

"The usual. Family gossip. A potluck
supper. It was held in the community hall,
and cousin Joe played the piano and
sang. He was the only one interested in
the Republic of Crowmania." Then she
asked the inevitable question: "How did
you like the macaroni and cheese?"

"I've never tasted its equal!" he said with
fervor and only a slight bending of the
truth.

On Tuesday morning no one could believe
it! The sun was shining, and the cessation
of the rain left a blessed void. Qwilleran
shouted just to hear his own voice: "Hallelu-
jah!" With restored ambition he dashed off
a thousand words about the dogcart races
and took it to the bank to be faxed. The
downtown streets swarmed with vacation-

ers in dark glasses—laughing and yelling and going into shops to spend money. There was no sign of Mildred's disaster.

Qwilleran had lunch at the Nasty Pasty, ordering the local specialty that was best when picked up in both hands. While enjoying his primitive repast, he thought of Owen's Place, open for lunch once again. Derek would be playing the efficient manager and friendly host, dressing the skewered potatoes at tableside with a theatrical flourish. At two o'clock he would be off-duty and going to Elizabeth's Magic to report.

Qwilleran opted to stay in town till then. He could say good-bye to the businessfolk he knew and listen to their worst-ever rain stories, taping them for use in the Friday "Qwill Pen":

"Didn't mind the wet, but the noise was like livin' in a wind tunnel."

"To make it worse, my dog howled all night."

"Whole family wore earplugs. Only way we could get any sleep."

"It was like living under Niagara Falls."

Qwilleran would open his column with the dictionary definition of rain: "water falling in drops condensed from vapor in the atmosphere. Also the descent of such drops. See: FOG, MIST."

Shortly after two o'clock he went to Elizabeth's to have Polly's vest gift wrapped. There were quite a few customers buying skewers and raving about the potatoes and the personable young man who dressed them at tableside. "There he is!" they cried when he burst in the front door. They applauded, and he bowed graciously before striding to the rear of the store.

Qwilleran followed. "How was the kick-off?"

"Great! There's nothing like a mystery or a scandal to attract customers. We had more orders for potatoes than we had skewers, so we cheated. We stuck skewers into ordinary baked potatoes. Nobody knew the difference."

"Was Ernie pleased with the turnout?"

"Sure was! And she was bug-eyed over the flowers from a well-wisher. I knew they were from you, but I didn't tell. I put them at the entrance on the maitre d's desk. They look swell!" Derek glanced toward the front of the store. "Here comes Bad News Barb.

Something's wrong with her; I think she's been jilted again—Don't be too sympathetic, Qwill; she goes for older men."

"How do you know?"

"We were in high school together, and she was always coming on to the science teacher, who was twice her age, and the principal, who was a grandfather."

The knitter walked solemnly toward the two men, carrying a box of goofy socks. "These need price tags," she said to Derek.

He took them into the stockroom, and Qwilleran asked her, "Do you knit vests for men? I wouldn't mind having one for myself in olive green—with some kind of interesting knit."

"There are lots of stitches," she said. "I could show you samples. Do you want me to dye some yarn samples, too?"

Before he could reply, there was a moment of silence in the store as the building vibrated. Then came a thunderous *boom* followed by crashing and screaming.

"Earthquake!" Derek yelled, charging out of the stockroom. "Get out! Get out! Everybody out!"

He ran through the store, waving his

arms and shoving customers toward the exit. There were cries of disbelief, bewilderment, fear.

"Stay calm!" Elizabeth shouted as she locked the cash drawer.

Oak Street was in turmoil. Frightened customers and workers streamed from the various stores and offices and huddled in the middle of the street, not knowing what had happened or where to run. On Main Street, half a block away, sirens were wailing and emergency vehicles with flashing blue lights were speeding eastward. From somewhere came an amplified voice of authority: "Evacuate all buildings! Police order! Evacuate all buildings!" The honking of medical and firefighting equipment added to the anxiety on Oak Street.

Then there were shouts of "Look! Look!" among the evacuees, and fingers pointed to the east where a cloud of dust or smoke billowed upward.

Qwilleran made a dash for Main Street with a double purpose: to identify the nature of the disaster and to phone the newspaper. He found official vehicles turning into Sandpit Road, while scores of individuals fled away from the Great Dune Motel and surrounding establishments. Yellow tape defining danger zones was stretched in all directions. He showed his press card to a deputy guarding the entry.

"Sorry, Mr. Q," she said. "Security orders."

"Is it an earthquake?"

"Sinkhole . . . Step aside, please." A sheriff's car with a dog cage in the backseat drove through.

Among the many flustered persons swarming up to Main Street was the antique dealer, and Qwilleran shouted, "Arnold! Where is it? Where's the sinkhole?"

"Back of the restaurant! Huge cave-in! Cars swallowed up!"

At the same time the earth rumbled like thunder, and the east end of the Great Dune crumbled, engulfing the rear of Owen's Place. Giant trees in full leaf, with enormous trunks and root systems, came tumbling end-over-end.

Qwilleran ran to his van and called the newspaper. Thank God, he thought, that the restaurant was closed! Then the question struck him: *Where was Ernie?*

In the milling crowd he spotted Derek,

head and shoulders above the rest. He yelled, "Derek! Was she in the RV?"

"I'm positive! I told the police! They took an S-and-R dog in!" He pushed his way through the crowd to Qwilleran's side.

"Was anyone working in the kitchen when you left?"

"The prep cook and the dishwasher. But I'm sure they'd get out when the pavement caved in, or the building began to shake . . . Ernie, though, went to the RV to plot the dinner procedure." Derek's face was pale and drawn. "The dog will find her, dead or alive. I wish I could be optimistic, but I've got this gut feeling that she's gone."

Qwilleran stroked his moustache with a heavy hand. "Let's go into the hotel for a cup of coffee."

In the coffee shop they sat in a dark booth instead of a sunny window overlooking the harbor; it seemed more appropriate. They sat weighted with silence for a while. Qwilleran was thinking about Mildred's rune stones and her prediction of disaster. Then he thought about Derek's loss. The young man admired Ernie tremendously, and they had developed a rapport. He had also lost a good position that would launch him on a serious career.

Finally Derek said, "I wish I'd taken a picture of Ernie in her chef's toque and that tunic with buttons on the side. It was neat! . . . She was so professional . . . I'm the only one in town who got to know her. I thought she was swell. So did the kitchen staff."

"Did she talk about her training?"

"Yeah. I asked her. She had two years at a good culinary institute. What a curriculum! Besides basic cooking she got to study baking and pastry arts, international cuisine, and nutrition. There were courses like knife skills, menu-planning, wine, purchasing, and I don't know what else. She wasn't stingy with her know-how either. She liked to teach. Do you know the two most important things in the chef business? Learning to taste, and learning to make a good sauce. That's what she said, anyway."

"Were you tempted to get into cooking?" Qwilleran asked.

"Nah. I like being out front, meeting people, and managing the service . . . Qwill, I can't believe she's gone!"

"Let's not give up hope. Miracles can happen."

The radio that provided country music and local commercials as background noise for the coffee shop was interrupted by a news bulletin.

"Turn it up!" Qwilleran yelled to the cashier:

"What was thought to be an earthquake in Mooseville this afternoon was the sudden opening of a deep sinkhole behind a restaurant on Sandpit Road, destroying two parked vehicles and causing a major sandslide at the east end of the Great Dune. When it occurred, the restaurant was closed to customers, but it's not known at this time whether the kitchen staff escaped. Police, fire, and rescue squads are at the scene."

Qwilleran, summing up what he had heard about the Bowens, was led to ask, "Do you think she really grieved about losing her husband?"

"Well . . . she went through the motions, but . . . I don't know."

"People grieve in different ways—some only in private, keeping up a brave front in public."

"Yeah, well, to tell the truth, I didn't get any good vibes between those two." Derek jumped up. "I should go and try to find Liz." He shuffled out of the coffee shop with none of the bursting energy that was his style.

18

When Derek left the coffee shop, Qwilleran suddenly remembered his dinner date with Polly . . . at Owen's Place! He paid for the coffee and phoned her from a public booth in the lobby. "Have you heard the news on WPKX?" he asked.

"I haven't been listening to the radio. What is it? Not too bad, I hope."

"Very bad. A sinkhole behind the restaurant where we were supposed to have dinner! And it caused a catastrophic sandslide—the east end of the Great Dune."

"Qwill! I can't believe this!" she said in horror. "Are you exaggerating?"

"Not at all. I was there when it happened. I was on Oak Street, a block away."

"I hope there was no loss of life."

"That hasn't been announced, but I have fears for the chef—a young, talented, dedicated woman."

"How dreadful!"

"So where shall we have dinner? I haven't had time to move back to Pickax as yet, but I could pick you up, and we could go to the Old Stone Mill, or Tipsy's Tavern."

"I don't know, Qwill . . . This is such depressing news! Do you mean the Great Dune itself is destroyed?"

"Tons of it! Trees and all!"

There was a pause at the Indian Village end of the line. "Perhaps we should postpone it until tomorrow night. I go back to work tomorrow, and you could pick me up at the library."

"And I'm definitely moving back to Pickax tomorrow morning. I'll call you at the library as soon as I get in."

With that matter settled, Qwilleran went out on Main Street again—to listen. The tourists were concerned only with the disruption of their vacations, but the locals had explanations to exchange. They blamed the sand-mining that was unwisely contracted during the Great Depression . . . the local commissioners for steadfastly ignoring the potential dangers . . . the short-sighted taxpayers who voted down a safety study . . . interplanetary Visitors for tampering with the weather and causing the abnormal rain . . . and greedy developers who had enraged the Sand Giant.

For news-on-the-hour, Qwilleran returned to his van and tuned in WPKX. He heard this:

"One casualty has been reported in the Mooseville disaster. Ernestine Bowen was killed in her recreation vehicle when it dropped into the sinkhole and was burried under tons of sand. She was the chef at Owen's Place. Her husband disappeared a week ago in a freak accident on the lake. The couple had come from Florida to open a restaurant for the summer."

Parked near Qwilleran's vehicle was John Bushland's green van. The photographer was obviously getting ground photos while aerial shots were being taken from the hovering helicopter. Qwilleran wrote a note on the back of his business card and wedged it under Bushy's windshield wiper. Then he spotted Phil Scotten in the crowd and said, "Did the boats go out today?"

"They went, but got a late start," the fisherman said. "I don't work the boats every day; I do the accounting for the fisheries. I heard the news on the air and had to come and see for myself. Never thought it would happen—not in my lifetime, anyway."

Qwilleran nodded soberly. "The sheriff's dog was on the job, and a victim was found in the rubble."

"That's Dutch, a German shepherd, trained for search-and-rescue. He's highly intelligent, has a good sense of sight and smell, and *never gives up*! That's the beauty of an S-and-R. Einstein is trained as an all-purpose dog. In his five-year career he sniffed out millions of dollars' worth of contraband. But all they need around here is an S-and-R. Dutch found a deer-hunter who went into the woods alone, tripped, and broke a leg . . . and he found an old lady who wandered away from Safe Harbor in a snowstorm."

Qwilleran said, "If I had a dog, it would be a German shepherd."

"You couldn't do any better than a shep. Remember the bloody riot at the soccer game between Sawdust City and Lockmaster? After that, Dutch and his handler attended the games and—no more trouble! The dog's presence alone was enough to keep the enthusiasm within bounds. My old college roommate Down Below is a handler on a police force, and I'll tell him to watch for a shep going into retirement, if you want me to."

"Uh . . . do that!"

"Are you covering the disaster for the newspaper?"

"No, I was here when it happened. I've been waiting for them to open the lake highway to eastbound traffic."

When Qwilleran arrived at the cabin, the Siamese met him with expressions of concern; they knew something was wrong.

"Bad scene down there," he told them. "There's nothing we can do to help, so we're heading for home first thing in the morning."

He fed them and gave them a good

brushing to calm their apprehensions. They were basking in the late afternoon sun on the porch when the green van pulled into the clearing.

Bushy jumped out, waving the card. Qwilleran had written: "Good for G and T at the K ranch. Signed: Q."

"I need one," Bushy said. "I've exposed a lot of film in the last hour. They're giving the story most of the front page tomorrow, and most of the picture page."

"Well, I've got the gin and tonic. Have you got the lens?"

"I've got the lens. Have you got the cats?"

"They're on the porch in the sun, freshly fed and brushed, so they should be receptive. We'll take our drinks out there and talk about anything but cats and cameras. Don't even think about taking a picture; they read minds."

The two men took porch chairs facing the lake. To their left, visible from the corner of an eye, were the Siamese: Koko striking aristocratic poses on his pedestal; Yum Yum stretched full-length on the warm glass top of the snack table.

Bushy asked, "Where were you when it happened?"

"At Elizabeth's Magic. They thought it was an earthquake, and we rushed out into the street. We saw the dune collapse."

"It buried the rear of the restaurant and killed the chef," Bushy said, "and—strange enough—it was her husband who disappeared in his boat a week ago. I have a theory about that."

"So have I," said Qwilleran. "It was his boat that was in conference with *Fast Mama*, the day you and I were out on the lake. I say there's got to be some connection."

"I say it was an abduction. Do you know, Qwill, that Mooseville has an ordinance on the books going back more than a hundred years—an ordinance about UFOs? It's never been enforced and never been rescinded."

"What's the nature of it?"

"Anyone having contact with a 'flying boat' must report the incident to the town constable within twenty-four hours. Would they have enacted such a law if there hadn't been any 'flying boats' in the sky?"

"Well . . ." Qwilleran thought, How can I tell him that his ancestors weren't quite sane? He said, "How did you find out about it?"

"My grandfather told me when I was a kid. He'd seen several flying boats himself, when out with the fishing fleet. Recently I got the . . . idea of . . ." His voice trailed off. He stood up slowly, raised his camera, and clicked it while facing the lake.

Qwilleran turned his head cautiously. Yum Yum was lounging on the table, and nestled between her forelegs was Gertrude with a tipsy expression embroidered on her calico face. Yum Yum, without knowing it, was facing the camera with a contented look of fulfilled motherhood.

"That does it!" Bushy announced with satisfaction. "If that doesn't win a prize, I'm going to give up photography."

"What about Koko?" Qwilleran asked.

"Forget that tyrant! He's missed his chance. He'll never be famous."

Having heard the click-click-click, Koko had jumped from the pedestal to the floor and—as the poet delicately phrased it— was kicking up behind.

Qwilleran said to him, "I'm going to trade you in on a German shepherd!"

Wednesday was moving day, and the sooner they left the cabin, the better Qwilleran would like it. Packing had to be done surreptitiously; although Koko was usually eager to jump into the carrier, the sight of it sent Yum Yum scurrying to places unknown. Once she was found on the top shelf of the pantry, behind the supply of paper towels; another time it was under the red blanket in the bunkroom, where she flattened herself like an omelette; then again she turned up among the wires behind the stereo amplifier. Qwilleran's strategy was to lock them on the lake porch until the van was loaded, then grab Yum Yum and pop her into the carrier before she knew what day it was.

On this occasion she was captured and caged, but Koko—instead of panting to join the expedition—vanished suddenly and utterly, like the legendary *Jenny Lee*. Impatiently, Qwilleran checked all possible hiding places while Yum Yum's wailing in the carrier added to his frustration. He yelled "Treat!" That was a password guaranteed to bring Koko stampeding into view. Instead, there was only a faint murmur in the upper reaches of the cabin. Twenty feet above the floor, in the peak of the roof, the cat had elongated himself on a narrow shelf created by the ridgepole and rafters.

After shouting the magic word again and hearing another nonchalant murmur, Qwilleran sat down to think. There was no ladder in the toolshed capable of reaching the peak. He was reluctant to call out the volunteer firefighters on such a mission. At that moment the phone rang, and he answered with a curt "Yes?"

It was Polly, sounding frantic. "Qwill, I'm back at work and calling an emergency meeting of the library board tonight. We have a mess on our hands."

Grouchily, he muttered, "Did Mac and Katie throw up?" They were newly acquired library cats.

Ignoring the feeble quip, she said, "My assistant has resigned; the new roof is leaking; and someone tore a page from Webster's Unabridged! We'll have to postpone our dinner date again."

"I was getting the message."

"Are you moving back to the barn today?"

"That was my intention, but we have a crisis here, too. I'll keep in touch."

Replacing the receiver, he heard a *thump, thump, THUMP* as Koko descended from his perch in three stages. Back on the floor he licked his right paw calmly and thoroughly.

"Okay, young man, you've had your little joke. Now let's go!"

As Qwilleran rattled the latch of the carrier, the phone rang again, and Koko flew up to the peak of the roof as if jet-propelled.

This time it was Junior Goodwinter, speaking in a muffled voice that suggested matters of great secrecy. "Qwill, how are you coming with Operation Uno What?"

"Slowly and painfully."

"Could you meet today's deadline? A hole just opened up on page five. Somebody killed an ad."

"Will it blow my cover if I fax it? Who's in charge of the fax machine?"

"Wilfred. Use an alias. Use a Fishport address . . . Thanks a lot, Qwill."

Qwilleran hurried to the van and retrieved his typewriter. Then, releasing Yum

Yum from the carrier and forgetting about Koko, he pounded out three pages of copy:

Dear sweet readers—Your charming, sincere, intelligent letters warm Ms. Gramma's pluperfect heart! Sorry to hear you're having trouble with the L-words. The safest way to cope with *lie, lay, lied, laid* and *lain* is to avoid them entirely. Simply say, "The hen deposited an egg . . . He fibbed to his boss . . . She stretched out on the couch." Get the idea? But if you really want to wrestle these pesky verbs to the mat, use Ms. Gramma's quick-and-easy guide:

1—Today the hen *lays* an egg. Yesterday she *laid* an egg. She *has laid* eggs all summer. (Ms. Gramma likes them poached, with Canadian bacon and Hollandaise sauce.)

2—Today you *lie* to your boss. Yesterday you *lied* to him. You *have lied* to the old buzzard frequently. (Tomorrow you may be fired.)

3—Today you *lie* down for a nap. Yesterday you *lay* down for a nap. In the past you *have lain* down frequently. (See your doctor, honey. It could be an iron deficiency.)

There was more. Ms. Gramma tackles such bothersome partners as who-and-whom, that-and-which, as-and-like, and less-and-fewer. And the copy made it to the fax machine on time.

After that ordeal, Qwilleran treated himself to a pasty for lunch and reviewed his two-week "vacation." He had intended to stay in Mooseville a month, but any more "vacation" would knock him for a loop, he decided. There had been no time to walk on the beach or ride the recumbent bike or entertain the cats with *The Celebrated Jumping Frog of Calaveras County*. There had been one incident after another, and a tremor on his upper lip convinced him there were more to come. Perhaps Koko had sensed some forthcoming development and was trying to stop him from leaving the sea.

Before returning to the cabin, he visited Elizabeth's Magic for a disaster update. She was alone. "My customers are all gawking at the sandslide. People like to be horrified when it's someone else's horror."

"Where's Derek?"

"He was grieving about Ernie and about

LILIAN JACKSON BRAUN

the loss of his job, so I told him to take a long walk; that always helps . . . What about you, Qwill?"

"I'm still interested in an olive green vest, but I want to see color samples."

"Barb was here a few minutes ago but left when she found Derek wasn't here. She's one of his groupies, you know, and I suspect Ernie was trending in that direction." Elizabeth arched her eyebrows. "After her husband died, she wanted Derek at the hotel for daily conferences."

"Your guy has a magnetic personality. Devoted females will always be hanging around the stage door. You'll have to get used to it," he advised. Cynically he thought, Elizabeth had nothing to fear; Derek knows which side his bread is buttered on . . . or, as Ms. Gramma would say, on which side his bread is buttered.

"Did Polly like her vest?" she asked.

"She hasn't seen it. We were supposed to have dinner at Owen's Place last night."

"When the library is ready, do you suppose she'd cut the ribbon for us on opening day? The head of the county library seems more appropriate than a politician who's running for office."

"And better looking, too," he said. "Are you planning to have a library cat?"

"I hadn't thought of it, but what a splendid idea!"

"They have all kinds at the animal shelter. Pick one that looks literary, and have a contest to name him or her."

Qwilleran walked back to Main Street, where his van was parked. On the way he heard running footsteps behind him and a throaty voice calling, "Mr. Q! Mr. Q!" It was Barb Ogilvie, considerably more alive than she had been recently.

"Elizabeth and I were just talking about you and my olive green vest," he said.

"I'll dye some yarn samples as soon as I get back on track," she said. "I've had a bad time."

"Sorry to hear that."

Swiveling her glances from side to side (she seldom looked anyone directly in the eye), she said, "I don't want to impose, Mr. Q, but I wish I could talk to you a bit—about something serious."

He huffed into his moustache. Young females were always confiding in him, and he was tired of the kindly-uncle role. "If you're looking for free advice, don't expect any from me," he said, adding lightly, "unless you sign a release promising not to sue."

Barb gestured helplessly. "I just want to unload, and you're the only one I know who's cool enough to understand."

The compliment, coupled with his unbridled curiosity, led him to suggest talking over a cup of coffee somewhere.

She hesitated. "I don't dare . . . talk about it . . . in a public place."

He thought, If she expects an invitation to the cabin, it's no deal! Then he had an inspiration! "I've never seen the petroglyphs. You could give me a guided tour." He knew they were on the Ogilvie ranch. "It wouldn't be for a newspaper story—just for my own education."

She hesitated. "It would have to be when Alice isn't at home, like . . . this afternoon?"

"Four o'clock?" he suggested.

"Wear boots. It could be muddy."

19

When Qwilleran drove into the Ogilvie farmyard at four o'clock, Barb met him and told him where to park. "My dad's pleased to know you want to see the 'glyph garden," she said. "He reads your column, and he met you once at Scottish Night in Pickax. He says you wore a kilt and made a great speech."

"Why didn't you want your mother here, if I may ask?"

"Oh . . . she'd want to go with us. She has to stick her nose in everything."

The driveway tapered into a rough wagon trail and then into a footpath. "Nice day for a hike," he said. "May I carry the tote bag?" It contained two colorful seat cushions from the porch furniture.

"We'll want to sit on the stones, and they're damp," she said. "I often go down there to knit. Is that crazy?"

"Not at all. I imagine it's quiet."

"Not really. I take a boom box."

"In that case, if I have a choice, I'd like my vest to be knitted under the influence of Dizzy Gillespie and Charlie Parker."

They tramped across pastures, through the gates of numerous fences, and past grazing flocks. "What are the petroglyphs doing on your land?" he asked. He knew the answer, but she enjoyed explaining how the lake had shrunk in the last few thousand years. "The shoreline that's two miles away was once *right here*, so the 'glyphs were on the beach. I don't know who put them here—probably the Sand Giant."

The trail ended at a high chain-link fence enclosing a clutter of large flat slabs . . . and a colony of crows.

"This looks like the Republic of Crowmania in parliamentary session," Qwilleran said.

"They know me. I usually bring them a handful of corn. Today I forgot . . . Do you want to poke around the stones for a while? There's not much to see—just chicken scratchings that are supposed to be some kind of secret language."

"Then I suggest we get down to business."

They selected two fairly horizontal slabs and sat on the red-and-white striped cushions.

"Mind if I smoke?" Barb asked, taking cigarettes from the tote bag.

"Yes, I mind," Qwilleran said, "but for your sake, not necessarily mine."

With a roguish glance, she said, "You sound just like my parents."

"Then there are three smart people around here," he said . . . Now what did you want to tell me?" He was in a snappish mood.

Reluctantly she dropped the cigarette pack into the tote bag. "I don't know where to begin."

"As the King of Hearts said to the White Rabbit, begin at the beginning and go on till you come to the end, then stop."

"Well . . . I told you about Florida and

the balloon-chaser, didn't I? After I chalked him off, I started dating my boss. He was a lot older, but we had fun. He took me out on his boat, and I think he really liked me. I liked my job, too."

"Where were you working?"

"At his restaurant. The only trouble was—the other waitresses were jealous. The boss gave me the best tables, and I was in solid with the chef. That meant my orders were filled first, and my customers got little extras, so I got bigger tips . . . Do you know?—a guy once left me a big tip and then went to the restroom, and I saw his date swipe it!"

Qwilleran huffed into his moustache. "Nothing surprises me. Stick to your story."

"Well . . . one day another waitress backed me into a corner and said, 'We all know what's goin' on, honey, and you'd better quit this job *right now* or we'll tell his wife, and she'll come after you with a cleaver!' . . . His wife! She was the chef! I thought he was a bachelor! I thought they were brother and sister! How could I be so dumb?"

"It happens," he said.

"I decided in a hurry that Florida was a

dead end for me. I came home and started being a country girl again."

"How long ago was that?"

"A year ago last winter. I started knitting seriously, and everything was okay until this summer, and then they suddenly showed up in Mooseville—the Bowens!"

"Did they know you lived here?"

"I guess I talked about my hometown a lot when I was Down Below. I always told people about the nice summer temperature in Moose County. Summers down there were unbearable!"

"Did Owen try to contact you?"

"No, and I stayed away from Sandpit Road! Then, after he died, Ernie called the ranch and wanted me to have dinner with her at the hotel. She said I was the only person she knew within two thousand miles. So I went to her suite. She had two dinners sent up and champagne in an ice bucket. It was neat! She threw her arms around me and cried a bit, and I got sort of choked up, too. At first we just talked about Florida. When they decided to come up here, she drove the convertible, and Owen drove the RV, towing the *Suncatcher*. She really didn't care for boats, but he said they should take a picnic cruise on their day off, or people would talk . . . God! I need a cigarette!"

There had been times in Qwilleran's life when he needed a smoke or a drink—desperately—so he said, "Go ahead. I'll walk around and look at the chicken scratchings."

When Barb was revived and had carefully buried the evidence, she returned to the conference area. "Alice comes down here to check up on me," she explained.

"Do you smoke while you're knitting?"

"No. Never."

"That should tell you something," he said. "Knit more; smoke less; live longer."

"Yes, doctor," she said impudently.

"Now go on with your story."

"Well, on their first day off after opening the restaurant, they were out on the lake when a weird speedboat started following them and finally flagged them down."

Fat Mama, Qwilleran thought.

"Owen told them to buzz off. He said the *Suncatcher* was not for sale. But Ernie was suspicious. You can't live in Florida without knowing what goes on, drugwise, and she had seen some locked suitcases down in the cabin. She started asking innocent questions and pretended not to be shocked by the answers. Putting two and two together, she figured that Owen had a commission from a Florida drug ring and was supposed to open up a new market in an area that was ripe for it. He told her to keep her eyes shut and her mouth shut, and it would be the best investment she ever made. If she didn't, he told her, she'd never cook another meal. He was quite cool about it."

"What did she do?"

"What *could* she do?" Barb said. "She didn't want to be a dead chef. But if she kept her mouth shut, wouldn't that make her an accomplice? She had nightmares about cooking vats of oatmeal in a prison kitchen. It was driving her crazy. She started making mistakes at the restaurant."

"I heard about the mistakes," Qwilleran said. "Derek was concerned about her. He thought she was worried about Owen's drinking. There were two theories about his death. A lot of people thought he was crocked and fell overboard."

"I know, but Ernie told me she'd made a

deal with the devil. Owen would put her through chef's school, and she'd run his restaurant. All she ever wanted in life was to work with food, supervise a kitchen, train a staff, and wear a chef's toque. She didn't care if he drank a fifth a day and chased women. She hoped he'd die of cirrhosis, and the restaurant would be hers. Suddenly she got an idea that would get her off the hook with Owen, and she could start her own business—with Derek as a partner." She stopped and gulped. "I need another cigarette . . . Please!"

"Go ahead." Qwilleran took another turn around the enclosure. He even talked to the crows in their own language, cawing the way Koko did, but they ignored him.

After the ritual of burying the butt, Barb was ready to talk. "This isn't easy to talk about," she said. "Ernie should never have told me. But I need to get it off my mind."

"I'm listening," he said in a tone more sympathetic than he had been using.

"It was their second day off. There aren't many pleasure boats around on a Monday, and Owen said they wouldn't be bothered by customers from Bixby because the deal was: Never on Monday. He said some stupid guy had got his signals crossed the week before . . . So they anchored at Pirate Shoals. Ernie ate her lunch, and Owen drank his. She chattered about new items she wanted to put on the menu, and finally Owen flaked out on the banquette in the stern. As soon as he started snoring, she got a potato skewer from the picnic basket and stabbed him in the ear. Then rolled him over the railing."

There was silence in the 'glyph garden. Even the crows were quiet.

After a while, Qwilleran said, "Wouldn't there be a lot of blood—from an artery?"

"She sopped it up with towels and stuffed them in the bait bucket. Then she threw it overboard, along with the locked suitcases. She moved the boat about a mile before calling for help."

"One question, Barb. Why did she tell you all this? Why didn't she keep her grisly little secret?"

"I don't know. We'd drunk two bottles of champagne, and she conked out on the bed. I wasn't in any condition to drive, so I flopped on the sofa. I woke up early in the morning and went home . . . God! What had she done to me? I didn't know what to do! There was no one I could ask for advice. Which is worse? To betray someone who trusts you? Or to be a party to murder? I went around like a zombie for a week, and then—"

"And then the Sand Giant came to your rescue," Qwilleran said, "except that you have information on a homicide that could enable police to effect a closure, and it's your social duty to report it . . . Do you know anyone in the sheriff's department?"

"Deputy Greenleaf. We were in high school together."

"Tell her the whole story, and she'll tell you what to do. Mention Pirate Shoals as the scene of the alleged crime. Then the sheriff and SBI will investigate as they see fit."

"One thing I'm thankful for," Barb said. "She wasn't one of us."

A commotion among the crows—frenzied cawing, fluttering, and squabbling—signaled the end of the conversation.

Arriving at the cabin, Qwilleran found all five skewers hanging on their brads. Either Koko was tired of his new toy, or it was his way of saying "case closed." The cat was now lounging contentedly in a patch of sunlight coming through a roof window. Qwilleran thought of the poet's Jeoffrey: *For there is nothing sweeter than his peace when at rest.*

20

After feeding the Siamese, Qwilleran opened the lakeside door, and the three of them moved gratefully onto the porch with its late-afternoon sun, friendly breezes, and idyllic view. "This is your last chance, guys, to watch the twilight bird ballet and the nighttime show of stars!"

"Yow!" said Koko.

"And as for you, young man, you're going back to Pickax tomorrow, even if we have to bring in the fire department with a hose!"

At that moment the cat's ears pricked,

and he turned his head toward the cabin interior. In a few seconds the phone rang.

It was Lisa Compton. "Are you busy, Qwill? Do you have company?"

"I have some four-legged company, and we're busy watching the crows. What did you have in mind?"

"Well, Lyle has a new toy he wants to show you. He thinks you'll want one like it. Do you mind if we walk over there?"

"Come along. We'll have a farewell drink. I'm leaving tomorrow."

Five minutes before the Comptons arrived, Koko knew they were on the way. When they came into sight, Lyle was shouldering a long tubular carrying case.

Qwilleran went to the top of the sand-ladder to greet them. "Don't tell me! It's a shotgun," he guessed.

After they were seated on the porch, and after the drinks were served, Lyle unsheathed a brass telescope about a yard long, together with an extendable tripod in wood with brass fittings.

"Handsome piece of equipment," the host said.

"You should get one, Qwill. It's great for

watching UFOs. What looks like a fuzzy green blob becomes a flying machine!"

"You're selling to the wrong customer, Lyle. I can't even see the fuzzy green blobs."

"Well, anyway, let me show you how powerful it is."

The three of them trooped to the small open deck that surrounded the screened porch. The tripod was extended to shoulder-height, and the telescope was trained on the lake.

"How does this compare with the Hubbell space 'scope?" Qwilleran asked.

"Considering the difference in cost, it does a pretty good job. Take a squint at that cabin cruiser out there."

Qwilleran squinted. "There are two couples having cocktails on deck . . . I believe they're drinking martinis."

"With anchovy olives or pickled onions?" Lyle asked.

"Seriously, Lyle, I'm impressed," Qwilleran said, "although I haven't caught the UFO bug myself. But you'll have fun with it."

They returned to the screened porch, and Lisa asked about Polly's vacation. She and her husband frequently traveled in

Canada. She said, "I hope Polly brings you something nice. They have wonderful cashmeres there—from Scotland."

"One of her postcards says she's bringing me a loonie and a toonie, whatever they are."

"They're coins that replace paper money," Lyle said, "and I'm all in favor of the idea. The loonie has a loon on one side and is worth a buck. The toonie is worth two bucks. Both are about the size of our half-dollar, but those clever Canadians have put a copper center in one and a faceted edge on the other."

Lisa said, "We have more than two hundred color slides of our trips to Canada, and we'd love to show them to you and Polly some weekend."

"That's something to look forward to," Qwilleran murmured in a minor key, already plotting a way to avoid the invitation. They were wonderful people—the Comptons—but . . .

Qwilleran read to the Siamese until the light began to fade. He enjoyed twilight, those moody moments between light and dark. What poet had called it *l'heure bleu*?

Polly would know. He missed her for reasons he had never put into words: her loving smile, soft voice, merry laugh—and
their shared interests. There would be
much to talk about over dinner at the Old
Stone Mill: her trip abroad and his adventures at home. He would not, however,
bring up the subject of Ernie's confession
to Barb; that was reserved for Andrew
Brodie, along with Koko's involvement in
the case. Only the police chief was privy to
the cat's unique talents, and even he was
skeptical.

Soon Qwilleran would invite Andy to the
barn for a nightcap and relate how Koko
knew instinctively that the body of the backpacker was buried in the sand ridge . . . and
how the cat knew when someone was
walking on the beach a quarter-mile
away . . . and how his catly strategy had
twice stopped Qwilleran from leaving Mooseville, when it was advantageous to stay.

Koko never used his powers frivo-
lously; he provided no clue to the "something nice" that Polly would bring
from Canada: a Shakespeare sweatshirt,
perhaps, or an unabridged reading of
Hamlet on cassettes.

Darkness always came reluctantly to the lake and its endless dome of sky, but eventually it was total. Qwilleran turned off the lights indoors and out, and the three of them sat listening to bullfrogs in a distant pond, an army of crickets, and waves lapping lazily on the shore. It was a moonless night but clear, and Koko studied the stars from his pedestal, while Yum Yum stared into the shrubbery and Qwilleran, stretched in his lounge chair, let his thoughts drift. All three were so enthralled by the magic of the night that they forgot the eleven o'clock curfew and stayed on the porch until well after midnight.

It was then that an uncanny incident occurred—something Qwilleran would later record in his personal journal. When it happened, he was too unnerved to write about it. He paced the floor, unable to sleep, and in the morning he was dressed and ready to leave the cabin even before feeding the cats. Before they were really awake, he stuffed them into the carrier and took them to the van. Luggage, coffeemaker, bike, and so forth were already loaded, and they took off for Pickax. Qwilleran was introspective, and the Siamese respected his mood. There was no yowling or jostling in the backseat.

At the barn, after a phone call to Polly confirming their dinner date, he felt better. He reserved their favorite table and then spent some time deciding what to wear. For three weeks he had lived in shorts, polo shirts, and sandals, and it was not easy to shift gears. There was no dress code at the Old Stone Mill, but customers paid the restaurant the compliment of dressing nicely.

At six o'clock he and Polly walked into the Mill, looking happy. Each carried a flat gift-wrapped package. Qwilleran thought hers was too small for a sweatshirt, too large for a CD, too flat for a piece of sculpture.

The hostess said, "We've missed you folks!"

"I've been vacationing in Canada," Polly said.

"I've been in the haunts of coot and hern," Qwilleran said.

"That's nice," said the hostess, smiling.

"See?" he said to Polly when they were

seated. "People don't listen. I could have said I'd been in jail."

First they toasted each other affection-ately—Polly with a glass of sherry, Qwilleran with Squunk water. Then he pre-sented his gift. A printed card inside said: "An original Barb Ogilvie design, hand-knitted in pointillé cale stitch, using un-bleached fleece from local sheep. The wool is hand-washed, hand-carded, and hand-spun on an antique wheel." Polly was thrilled.

When Qwilleran opened his souvenir of Canada, he did it gingerly, as if suspecting a package bomb.

"It won't bite," Polly said. "I had it muz-zled."

It was something made of fabric. It was in the Mackintosh clan tartan. It was a vest!

"Now we have a vested interest in each other," he said.

The humor of the situation tickled them both, and the dinner was off to a rollicking start. First Qwilleran wanted to know about the French-Canadian professor.

"He was so kind, so helpful, so gracious!" Polly said. "I invited him to visit Moose County."

"Does he speak English?" The question was facetious, of course.

"He speaks four languages. He's working on a book dealing with Canadian influence on northern communities in the U.S. Many of our early settlers came from Ontario, you know."

"That's not all we got from Canada," he said, recalling tales of Prohibition days.

Polly, for her part, wanted to hear about the Rainstorm of the Century that had led to the disaster on Sandpit Road.

He said, "Do you know the legend of the Sand Giant?"

"Yes indeed! It's my theory that it was inspired by a Scottish phenomenon. The Big Grey Man has been haunting a mountain in Scotland for at least two centuries."

Then Qwilleran mentioned the UFO library.

Polly knew about it. "The subject was brought up at the board meeting last night. It will be interesting to see what books they have. We have at least fifty titles in our collection, and some are checked out daily."

"Hmmm," he murmured in perplexity.

Twenty-four hours before, he would have scoffed at the fact.

Altogether, it was a memorable evening. When Polly was back in Indian Village and he was back in the barn, it was late, and he was sufficiently relaxed to write in his journal:

Pickax—Thursday, July 16
Last night was our last at the cabin. We were sitting on the porch after midnight with the lights turned off, indoors and out. To use a cliché, the night was pitch black. The cats like it that way; they're fascinated by the invisible sights and inaudible sounds that only they can see and hear.

When I'm lounging in a porch chair with my feet up, just thinking, time means nothing, so I didn't know how long I had sat there. The sky seemed to be getting lighter, yet my watch said it was only two-forty-five. The cats sensed something irregular and fussed nervously. Soon Yum Yum ran indoors.

Was it my imagination, or was the sky turning green? Also unusual was the deathlike silence. Suddenly a strong gust of wind stirred up papers and what-not on the porch, and Koko jumped on my lap and dug in with his claws for safety. It lasted only a few seconds, though.

At the same time a large round disc floated downward, throwing shafts of light on the beach. I could feel Koko's fur standing on end. His tail bushed. Next thing I knew, he was at the screened door, pawing the defective latch.

"Koko!" I yelled, though I couldn't hear my voice. I leaped out of my chair, but he was outside on the deck. I dashed after him and made a grab. He slipped away and headed for the beach, straight down the side of the dune.

Just as I was about to go after him, I saw small creatures tumbling out of the disc and sliding down the shafts of light. They had four legs and long tails! He was going to meet them!

"Koko!" I screamed, but no sound came out of my mouth. He was picking his way through the tall grass on the sandy slope. Desperate, I plunged headlong in a flying tackle and landed on top of him. For a second I saw stars, then blacked out.

When I came to my senses, I was pinned down under a heavy weight—in total darkness. Where was I? My eyes were open, but I couldn't see, and there was a throbbing in my chest that alarmed me.

Then something wet touched my nose. The weight on my body shifted. Managing to raise an arm, I felt fur! Koko was on my chest, purring loudly, and I was back in my lounge chair. How did I get there? My mind was muddled. The green light had disappeared, and the beach was dark. I could hear the waves splashing.

Still I felt stunned. It was a dream, I told myself . . . or was it? Koko's fur was sandy, and when I stood up, I brushed a shower of sand off my clothes.

It had been twenty-four hours after the incident before Qwilleran had finally found the objectivity to report it in his journal, and he still felt uneasy about the experience. He might be a fool, but he could not swear it was only a dream.

One thought haunted him and caused a spasm of discomfort in the roots of his moustache. Was this a clue to Koko's abnormal sensory perception? What were the cat's origins? No one knew. One day he simply . . . appeared.

Previously, Qwilleran had attributed Koko's superior intelligence to his sixty whiskers. Perhaps the secret was something more unthinkable—the intelligence of an alien race who were not little green men but little green cats!

As for Sixty Whiskers himself, he had not changed a whisker since the incident. He was still a handsome, intelligent, companionable, unpredictable, somewhat imperious, and frequently exasperating feline . . . But Qwilleran had changed. He was willing to concede that Koko was not seeing stars when he gazed at the sky; he was seeing fuzzy green blobs.